THE PENANCE

THE PENANCE

Fakir Mohan Senapati

Translated by
Snehaprava Das

BLACK EAGLE BOOKS
2019

BLACK EAGLE BOOKS

7464 Wisdom Lane
Dublin, OH 43016
E-mail: info@blackeaglebooks.org
Website: www.blackeaglebooks.org

First published in Odia as "Prayaschita" in 1915

First International Edition published by
BLACK EAGLE BOOKS, 2019

The Penance
by **Fakir Mohan Senapati**
Translated by **Snehaprava Das**

Copyright © 2019 by BLACK EAGLE BOOKS
Translation © 2019 by Snehaprava Das

Cover: Atul Bal
Interior Design: Ezy's Publication

ISBN- 978-1-64560-033-6 (Paperback)
Library of Congress Control Number: 2019953140

Printed in United States of America

To my parents
  - *Snehaprava*

Tales of Expiation: Introduction to Fakir Mohan Senapati's *Prayaschita*

Himansu S. Mohapatra

Prayaschita is the last of Fakir Mohan Senapati's four novels and the third and the last in his 'trilogy of crime and justice', to use the epithet coined by the eminent Senapati scholar John Boulton. The first two novels of the trilogy are *Chhamana Athaguntha* (1902 – English translation – *Six Acres and a Third*) and *Mamu* (1913 - English translation – *The Maternal* Uncle). *Prayaschita* was published in 1915, just three years before the death of the novelist. In the brief prefatory note affixed to the novel, the author says that he wrote it in a desperate hurry when he was in his sickbed. It was the painstaking revision and corrections by his young friend Pandit Kulamani Kabyatirtha, the headmaster of Balasore Training School that led to the book being published.

The novel does, of course, betray the signs of hasty composition. The spontaneity and freshness of Senapati's colloquial diction are glimpsed only intermittently. The prose is for the most part stilted. The garrulous narrator also called the 'touter-narrator', which is a trademark of Senapati's fictional writing, is all but absent. It is as if at the level of style also the novel is doing 'penance' for the comic exuberance and linguistic resourcefulness of the earlier novels, especially of *Chhamana Athaguntha*. In keeping with the Hindu philosophy of 'vanaprastha' or renunciation advocated – a bit too stridently in my opinion - in the novel's final chapters the style seems to have shed its usual playfulness, subtlety, and sophistication and taken on a somber and preachy quality. There is a distinct feeling that the author's best vein in prose fiction is done.

So, what does the novel have to recommend itself?

The novel is of value for the light it casts on Senapati's increasingly dark and tragic vision of life lived under the shadow of colonialism. He wrote it to defend the traditional values of the Hindu way of life which he saw as being gravely threatened by the alien value system of the British that had made huge inroads into the Indian society. In fact, it is a telling assault on the English education that is perforce mounted in the form of a defense of the traditional Indian society. Senapati has rightly chosen the form of the tragic novel for this purpose.

Prayaschita is tragic because the suffering depicted in it is gratuitous at worst or is grossly disproportionate to any crime or sin that may have been committed at best. For the crime or sin committed by both the father figures in the novel, Baisnab Charan Pattanaik Bidyadhar Mahapatra, the zamindar of Chandanpur, and Sankarsan Mohanty, the zamindar of Samsarpur, and the young protagonist Gobinda, the son of the former and the son-in-law of the latter, is that of hubris. Common to both the zamindars is the pride of possessing wealth and power. In addition, the former zamindar possesses caste pride, the pride of belonging to a pedigreed caste of Karanas known as Sri Karana. He has a touch of class which his rival, Sankarsan Mohanty, lacks because the latter's wealth is not inherited but is earned by the sweat of his own brow. In other words, Sankarsan Mohanty is an upstart. His sin consists in his wanting to gain acceptance into the so-called higher Sri Karana society. It is compounded by his manipulation of things to get his only daughter Indumati married to the only son of his rival to achieve the dual purpose of revenge and acceptance. And for the sins of the fathers, the children must pay and pay dearly. A case of mistaken identity leads to Gobinda being brutally beaten by the security guards of Sankarsan Mohanty and left for dead, his plan of a midnight romantic tryst with his beloved having boomeranged. The shaming and public humiliation of her husband lie heavily on Indumati's conscience, driving her to kill herself.

If ever there was a case of unmerited suffering, here is one. But then this is what tragedy is about. In this literary form the high and the mighty fall because of hubris or hamartia, but they rarely fall alone; they drag with them a whole host of innocent souls to their ruin. As the lines from *Hamlet* aptly put it, 'Never did/ The King sigh, but with a general groan.' Claudius and the Queen must die for their sins. But so must Hamlet and Ophelia. Likewise, Lear, Goneril, Reagan, and Edmund must die, but so must Cordelia. Yet if Lear can protest that he is more 'sinned against than sinning', then what is one to say of Ophelia or Cordelia? The case of Gobinda and Indumati is different. Not only are they innocent; they are objects or tools in other people's – and they are no other than their fathers - schemes. The justification the novel seems to offer for their suffering is that through this their respective parents can learn the folly of worldly pride and ambition. This echoes the story of *Romeo and Juliet*, but superficially. In Shakespeare's play, the death of the lovers can help establish peace and friendship between the Montague and Capulet families. The difference is that in the modern Odia version of this story only the female of the pair dies while the male lover lives on to do penance. The effect, of course, is the same: the feuding dynasties of Mahapatra and Mohanty find their way back to love and fostering care for which they are destined by dharma.

There is, of course, another explanation for the way things turn out in the novel. The novelist seems to be suggesting through this story of sin and repentance that it is English education which was responsible for the utter confusion of values in the traditional Odia society with Gobinda being presented as a stellar example of this confusion. Reading English books had made him stray in his early youth. The following lines from the letter of the reformed Gobinda to his doctor friend are indeed revealing:

But now I repent every moment for that. I don't know how reading a few English philosophical texts had made me so arrogant as to doubt the existence of God. What a foolish, ignorant fellow I was to believe the atheists who challenged the infinite power of the Supreme Soul, His endless mercy that spreads about in the whole cosmos. (Ch. 48)

The words are a stark acknowledgment of the fact that a Western outlook and the reading of English books, steeped in materialism and skepticism, had turned Gobinda into the hot-headed, selfish, myopic, pleasure-loving and ungrateful person he had become, causing him to lapse from the path of virtue and righteousness. And of course, behind this culture of atheism and hedonism, one can see the material base of the colonial dispensation that had made money the measure of all things, resulting in the decline of the aristocratic code of honor that governed a traditional land-owning class.

Sankarsan Mohanty is clearly a product of the colonial world of the cash-nexus, whereas Baisnab Charan Pattanayak Bidydhar Mahapatra is a representative of the pre-colonial world of personal pieties, affections and rites sanctioned by tradition. Their names echo their social role and function. Whereas the long double-barrelled name of the latter is suggestive of his charismatic larger than life status and aura, the ordinary and matter of fact name of the former typify his reduced status and the disenchanted and objectified world he lives in. The novelist's sympathy clearly lies with the former, as the pattern of contrast between the two clearly reveals. John Boulton does, in fact, see this as part of a wider pattern of the juxtaposition of good and evil that dominates Senapati's trilogy. As he says,

Fakir Mohan's novels contrast aristocrats like the Bagha Simhas of Ratanpur in *Chhamana Athaguntha*, Pratap Udit Malla in *Mamu* and Basinab Charana Mahapatra in *Prayaschita* with upstarts like Mangaraj in *Chhamana Athaguntha*, in Natabara Das in *Mamu* and Sankarsan Mohanty in *Prayaschita*. The aristocrat embodies the values of the old regime: the upstarts the materialism of the British rule.

This is, of course, true, but Fakir Mohan is also shrewd enough to perceive that in the new dispensation driven by money and cunning the day clearly belongs to the Mangarajas, Dases and Mohantys unless the traditional value system is reinforced.

The manipulation drama played out in the early section

of the novel, set in Cuttack, the colonial capital of Odisha, is a case in point. Who can forget the 'Feasting' chapter of the novel in which Darwin's theory of natural selection has been put to such ignoble, self-serving use by the plotters Sadananda and Rajiblochana? They quote Darwin's doctrine of mate selection, but their agenda is to nudge Gobinda insidiously towards an inter-caste marriage? Gobinda is gullible enough to take the bait with the tragic and catastrophic consequences we have seen. So, in writing the novel Senapati's objective is to exorcise those dark days, weeks and months at Cuttack, dominated by Darwin and other tools and ploys of colonialism.

The novelist wants to undo the wrong at two levels. First, at the level of the 'comeuppance plot' he shows Sankarsan Mohanty turned into 'Sankara', a mere 'golam' (servant), shorn of whatever power and glamour he had possessed at the beginning, a reversion precisely to the pejorative upper-caste terms that had attached to him and that he had rebelled against. Superimposed on this is the novel's 'redemptive plot' in which the entire cast of main characters, basically all the survivors of the tragedy, are taken through a rigorous course in self-purification or penance. This is how Senapati ensures the survival of the traditional Hindu way of life from the onslaughts of colonial modernity.

It is this civilizational aspect that tells *Prayaschita* as a tale of expiation from Charles Dickens's *Great Expectations* (1860), that other great tale of expiation to have come from English literature. For if we look at the plot trajectory of the two novels, we will find much in them that is comparable. Gobinda and Pip both set out to pursue their pleasures selfishly. Both become arrogant and ignore their benefactors. Both become snobs. And both receive their just deserts. The manner of their awakening is also similar, Pip burnt into insight and Gobinda beaten into it. Moreover, both get brain fever and go through a period of convalescence in the hospital during which they rise to new life and consciousness. Gobinda's transformation is, of course, more thoroughgoing than that of Pip. Pip dissociates himself from the industrial-capitalist society in the end only to become a stooge of the British Empire. Gobinda's soul searching leads him to reject the colonial baggage altogether, to search for his own roots and to spend the rest of his days, working for the good – and not 'profits', as in the case of Pip – of his community. Thus, in *Prayaschita*, his last novel, Senapati's comes home and declares his last will and testament.

■

Translator's Note

Between 1897 & 1915 Fakir Mohan Senapati wrote his four iconic novels, *Mamu, ChhaaMana Athaguntha, Prayaschitta,* and *Lacchama*. The first three, as most critical surveys on Fakir Mohan's works, point out, explore the socio-cultural realities during the eighteenth and nineteenth-century Odisha. They, in a way, fall in line with the novels written during those days in other Indian languages that conformed to the tradition of literary realism. While *Mamu* (The Maternal Uncle) moves on to examine different dimensions of familial and social relationships, *Chhamana Athaguntha* (Six Acres and A Third) narrativizes the exploitation of landless peasants by a rapacious feudal lord. The eponymous *Lacchama*, however, does not quite fit in the framework that holds the other three being more a historical romance than a realistic interpretation of a defective and despicable socio-cultural- economical l system inclined to oppress the weak and the underprivileged.

A more keen and meticulous study might incite the readers to discover a guiding element embedded in the inner consciousness of the major protagonists in the other three novels that sort of propels them to adopt vindictive and vicious methods to achieve their selfish ends. They could be viewed as extremists, lured either by a consuming ambition, or greed or a complex, a secret vendetta, an offshoot of an overpowering ego. Despite his total indifference to the sufferings of his own widowed sister and her sons, the devious Nazar Natabar, the maternal uncle (mamu) manages to manipulate the situation to suit his own selfish interest. His envy concealed under a visage of feigned concern for his nephews spells the height of hypocrisy. He might have been driven by a wounded ego feeling belittled before his brother-in-law's good reputation and economical status which perhaps got multiplied by his well-concealed disappointment in having a not so good-looking woman for a wife which he tries to overcome by a self- devised belief that her auspicious arrival has brought in good fortune to him. In *Chhaa mana Athaguntha* (Six Acres and A Third) the tyrant landlord Ramachandra Mangaraj swindles a fecund patch of land measuring six acres and a third out of the poor and trusting couple through sly machinations and subterfuge. These two great works reveal the author's enormous potential as a social satirist. One might be a little tempted to probe at some subliminal urge, if there be any, functioning as a motivating factor to guide the two protagonists to resort to such extreme measures for achieving their long-pursued goals. The inevitable conflict of interest that operates as the strongest leverage to set the action rolling forward in either a play or a fiction, as we all know, springs from either indomitable egocentricity or a sense of acute insecurity reflected in form of varied emotional upheavals. Thus, the propelling urge in *Mamu* may be identified as an inferiority complex transmuting into an irrepressible hatred and jealousy, while in the second one *Chhamana Athaguntha* it is sheer overwhelming greed and ambition to own something special and an egoistic conviction that to own a rich and fertile land is the prerogative of only a landlord. *Prayaschitta*, the third in this category of social satires, appears to be different in the very choice of its title. While the titles of the former two relate to a familial relationship (*Mamu* or The Maternal Uncle) and the measurement of a patch of land (Six Acres and a Third) respectively, *Prayaschitta* (The Penance) forthright relates to a state of mind, the working of the inner conscious. Penance usually results from a sense of guilt following an act of offense. Guilt is, as is defined in terms of psychology, an emotional experience that occurs when someone realizes or believes that his or her activity has violated a universal moral standard, upset a systemic orderliness and brought harm to an individual or individuals. The major characters in the said novel, as we find them, are obsessed with a sense of guilt and suffer a self-inflicted punishment to redeem their scarred souls. Like the other two, this novel also pictures a society lacerated with divisive forces like caste and class distinctions. The conflict of interest emanating from a clash of the superior ego of a higher sect of a particular caste and the wounded pride of a lower sect of the same caste generates a strong and sweeping current of envy and intolerance. The major characters which get pathetically caught in this turbulence of the warring passions are driven, though unintentionally, to commit certain acts to further intensify the conflict guiding the events in a path leading to a catastrophic climax. Govindchandra, the only son of the zamindar who belongs to a higher sect comes under the evil influence of a conniving friend who inspires him in the name of bringing reform into a system that writhes under the oppressive norms of tradition and conservatism. This scheming friend who belongs to the enemy camp persuades the idealistic youth to marry the daughter of the other zamindar belonging to the lower category of that caste without the knowledge of his father. The shocking revelation of truth shatters his parents. His mother falls ill and eventually succumbs to her illness. The young man caught in an unexpected circumstance as he pays a clandestine visit to his wife's place is mistaken for a bandit, beaten brutally and is carried in a palanquin to a hospital at Cuttack by his trusted vassal. The young woman, his wife, overwhelmed at the incident and feeling responsible since she has agreed to sign her name under a verse-letter written by her cousin, the very same fellow who lures the youth to this marriage, puts an end to her life by drowning herself. These two deaths of two innocent women pull forth the plot to its climax. The conflict which has until this point been external now gets internalized as the author shifts his focus from the conscious action to subconscious introspections. The two wealthy and powerful landlords moved by a self-condemnation decide to dissolve the ages-old enmity and relinquish their worldly lives. They leave for Vrindavan to settle there permanently as monks surrendering all their ego and pride at the Lord's holy feet. The young son of the zamindar, recovers from illness, is devastated on learning of the deaths of his mother and wife and driven by an acute sense of guilt and remorse leaves the hospital without informing the authorities and heads towards Varanasi to seek atonement for his evil deeds which, he believes, have destroyed two reputed families. His trusted servant who also has always been a dependable companion, heart-broken at this unexpected turn of events makes a frantic but futile search for his missing master and in the end, he too decides to abandon the worldly life and serve the Lord. He, like all others, arrives at Vrindavan and serves the two old zamindars now living a life of austerity without revealing his identity. At the end of the novel, all these major characters come together and repent for the respective roles they have played in bringing about the disaster. All they want is redemption through an act of rigorous penance. Thus, the two older monks, (the father and the father-in-law of young Govindchandra) advised him to return to the village and spend his life serving the tutelary deities of both the families. The companion maid of Govindachandra's dead bride, too, motivated by a sense of guilt that her friend has succeeded in her efforts of killing herself only because of sheer negligence on her (Marua's) part, decides to remain unmarried and dedicate herself to serving of the deities. Thus, at the end of the novel, we find all the characters have chosen the act of penance in different forms to absolve themselves of the sins they have knowingly or unknowingly committed. The plot of the novel evidently dwells more on the definition of the subliminal drives shaping the actions of the protagonists than outward circumstances.

On his observations on the novel, Prof Chintamani Acharya writes, (*Utkala Sahitya* 1916 vol 19, No-7) ......
'The degree of one's efficiency in interpreting human behavior in different contexts is often proportionate to his ability to delve into the human psyche. The fictionist must be adequately armed with the knowledge of the working of the human mind since the behavior and action of a man is influenced by it. In the absence of such observations, the delineation of characters and the plot development tend to lose their charm and are likely to be misconstrued.'

And again, in the same critique, 'A seasoned and skilled painter paints the less significant parts with equal precision as he does the major ones. He even takes meticulous care of the positioning of a dot or a line in his painting even though the viewer does not ordinarily miss them. In the novel *Prayaschitta,* the pictures of life painted in their minute details compels the reader to believe that the author-painter perhaps had experienced them first-hand.'

These are some remarkable comments by the great Fakir Mohan-critics that help define the author's versatility as a writer. He was at the same time a realistic observer and witty critic of the contemporaneous socio –a cultural-political scenario as well as an expert mind-reader. We discover an admirable synthesis of both these significant attributes in their finest forms in the present novel.

Translating Fakir Mohan in English is undoubtedly a challenging project. The task to capture and reproduce in English the author's witty phraseology expressed in regional dialects at times proves to be too demanding on a translator. The present English rendering of the novel has focused on negotiating the readability and translatability factors to produce a text that not just tries to approximate the style and theme of the original in a possible measure but to hold the interest of the reader of the recipient language. The rest is for the readers to decide.

- **Snehaprava Das**

CHAPTER - 1

It is hard to keep count of the number of legal disputes both the parties had raised.

Starting from the complaints lodged at the police station litigation followed endlessly from the lower court to the appellate court and finally to the High Court. There was, siding with each party, a crowd of lawyers, *mukhtars*, record-keepers, barristers and lesser employees of the court. The agents of both the parties, busy beyond belief, could not even find time to breathe. Tucking the puffy wallets under their arms cheerfully, they kept approaching the lawyers and other ministerial employees of their respective sides. Adding to the numerous civil lawsuits, strife among the men supporting each party were frequent occurrences in the village. Both were wealthy zamindars and men of unflinching arrogance and would prefer death to defeat. Since the borders of their estates touched, a cause to trigger a fight was always within easy reach.

The readers are sure to get confused unless they are told clearly about the root cause of all these disputes. The *pragana* of *Ashureswar* in the district of Cuttack was inhabited mostly by people of the *Karan* caste. The residents of the *taluka* of *Dashagrama* in this *pragana* belonged to a higher category of the caste known as *Srikarana*. The village of *Chandanpur* was exclusively a village of this higher category of the *Karanas*. Here in this village of Chandanpur stood the impressive-looking palace of the present *zamindar, Baishnaba Charan Pattanaik Bidyadhara Mahapatra.* A bitter conflict relating to the gradation of the status of the people of the caste had created quite an uproar during the time when his father late *Vishalakhya Pattnaik Bidyadhar Mahapatra,* was the *zamindar.* At that time, around sixty odd families in *taluka Dashagram* belonged to *Srikaran* caste. Now, including the subsequent generations, the count of the *Srikaran* households had gone beyond four hundred. They, however, acknowledged another sect called the *Odishi Karana* living in the same village as a second category of the *Srikarana* caste. According to the seniors and elders of the *Srikaranas,* the rest of the people bearing the surname Mahanty did not have the pure *Karana* blood in them; That they had acquired the privilege of introducing themselves as *Karanas* just through living together with the true Mahantys of the noble ancestry for years.

The *taluka* of *Samsharpur* was also a *Karana* dominated area. The inhabitants of this *taluka* also took pride in introducing themselves as *Srikaranas,* claiming themselves as the scions of the original pure Karana families whose descendants were spread throughout *Utkala* like branches of the original family tree. But the *Srikaranas* of *Dashagram* looked upon them as a sect of low-bred Karana caste and did not count them as their equal. The saying went that the name Golam Mahanty, a hybrid sect of *Karanas* continued to exist because many years before, the *Karanas* of *Samsharpur* had allegedly included a man with the surname *Mahanty* who was a lesser *Karana,* into their own caste by taking a bribe. The progenies of this man were known as the *Golam Mahantys.* Just like a pond that went by the name *Tala pokhari* probably because sometime in the past, a palm tree stood on its banks even though no trace of the tree is left now. This category of the hybrid *Karanas* was identified as the *Golam Mahantys* even in the present time.

The landlord, Zamindar *Samanta Baishnaba Charan Patnaik Bidyadhar Mahapatra* was quite a well-known figure in the district. In the past, his forefathers enjoyed the exclusive ownership of the sixteen acres of lands in *mouza Kisamat* in the *pragana of Ashureswar.* His late father, with an intention to become the head of the society of the *Srikaranas* of *Dakapur,* had permanently transferred the ownership of two acres of this land to the *Karana samantas* there. Since that time the *Karana samantas* had occupied the land and exercised their ownership on it for generations. They would continue to enjoy the right over it for all time to come since the transaction has been made legally effective by the District Court.

The zamindar of *Samsharpur* and the head of the *Karan*-society there, *Shankarshan Mahanty,* was an adventuresome, cunning and enterprising person. He did not have much ancestral property. He had traveled widely, tried his luck at several places and at several jobs. For quite some time, he had served in different British shipping companies in Calcutta. While supervising the loading and unloading of the consignments in the ships, he had earned quite a large sum of money by both fair and fraudulent means. He wheedled the sahibs to turn a blind eye to the misappropriation of the company's money. *Shankarshan Mahanty* made a lot of money in this way and became immensely rich in a short while. It was believed that the value of his self-acquired estate exceeds two lakh rupees. In addition to the large sum of interest-money he earned by lending grain and money to the villagers, he had hoarded a huge amount of unaccounted-for hard cash. It was also believed that *Mahanty* owned an equal measure of hidden property – kept away from prying eyes. People always sided with the men of money; though *Shankarshan Mahanty* was not the official head of the society of *Karanas*, the *Karana Samanta*s were always at his beck and call. The zamindar, too, was extremely generous towards his kinsmen. He had earned quite a reputation of being a kind and charitable person, a man who would not hesitate at all to give away everything to the distressed that seeks his help. He was widely acclaimed for this noble streak in his character.

The head of the *Karan* society of the *taluka Dashagram* used to hear the tales of the noble-natured zamindar of *taluka Samsharpur* grudgingly, his nostrils swollen in envy. Though it is true that the praise people shower on the zamindar of *Samsharpur* had never caused damage to the respectable status they themselves enjoyed, it was hard for the high-bred *Sri Karana* society-head to stomach the fact that a *Karan* of hybrid origin would earn such repute. Such intolerance did not behoove the philanthropic, devout and virtuous *Samanta Baishnaba Charan*. But alas, no man is perfect. However kinda man's nature might be, it is never free of a flaw, which like a dark spot spoils its cleanliness. The head of the *Karan* society in *Ashureswar pragana*, *Samanta Baishnaba Charan* considered himself a priceless gem of the *Karana* clan. He believed that society owed all its name and fame to him. *Shankarshan Mahanty* may be a zamindar or a man of great wealth but he remained a *Karana* of a base category. It was not easy to tolerate the commendation of such a person.

But for a small snag in it, *zamindar Sankarshan Mahanty*'s life seemed complete in all aspects. An obsessive desire to belong to the *Srikarana* society haunted him relentlessly. He was prepared to go to any lengths to achieve his end. He had a strong belief that nothing is unattainable to one who is ready to part with good money. Being a cunning man, he had managed to make several *Srikaran*s join his camp. But he did not fully rely upon the loyalty these people professed they had for him. They could not ensure him a position in the *Srikaran* society. They were opportunists and might, at any point in time betray his trust. It was the approval of the society-head *Baishnaba Charana Bidyadhar Mahapatra* that really counted. Hence, he had won over the goodwill of some of the senior *Srikaran*s, who he was confident, could influence their society-head in his favor.

On one pleasant afternoon the *zamindar, Baishnaba Charana Patnaik Bidyadhara Mahapatra* sat along with some of his close acquaintances on the porch of his court hall, relaxing, engaged in light, idle talks. A senior *Karana Sumanta* finding the atmosphere conducive to bring up the topic said, "What is the harm in taking *zamindar Sankarshan Mahanty* into the fold of our *Karan* society? After all, he is also *Karan* by caste." The suggestion instantly sparked off the society head's displeasure. Hiding his repugnance under a stiff, crooked smile he returned, "My dear B*hai Sa'nte*! You are such a senior person in our society. Does it behoove you to make such preposterous suggestions? Do you mean to say that we, the high-bred *Srikaranas* will sit together with the *Golam karana*s in their courtyard and share a meal with them? How absurd!! Enough is enough. Let's stop debating on this point."

Shankarshan Mahanty's grapevine, always alert and active, transmitted the news to him without delay. The egoistic zamindar *Baishnaba Charana Bidydhar's* rodomontade hit his own ego in such a degree that he could not control his anger. It is true that every man however noble has a flaw, great or small, in his character. *Sankarshan Mahanty*, too, was no exception. The man, despite his saintly attributes, was hot-tempered. Once he picked up enmity with somebody, he would not rest until he sent his opponent to their ruins. He stood up angrily and casting a hard glance at his associates and friends who sat nearby declared with an audacious vehemence, "Listen up all *Karana Samantas* here! I take a vow that I will destroy the person. All this property I own is self-acquired. I have earned it through my industry, enterprise, and perseverance. There is more than one lakh rupees of hard cash in my treasury and I have invested near about five lakh rupees in the money-lending business. Besides this, there is a granary stuffed with crops and my large estate. I will put all this at stake to fight a legal battle with that arrogant man to prove my status in the society. All of you stand witness to this resolve of mine."

The villages of both *talukas* lay adjacent to one another. Since their borders touched, incitements always came easily, creating wrangles and ructions among the villagers. A tiny issue was often blown out of proportion to raise a serious dispute. In a short span of time, many lawsuits, both legal and criminal, were filed by the villagers belonging to both *taluka*s. Caught in the crossfire of the battle between their mighty masters the interests of the poor innocent villagers were pathetically sacrificed.

CHAPTER - 2
ENGLISH-LEARNING

Samanta Baishnaba Charan Pattnaik had to come to Cuttack oftentimes to attend to legal and official matters. On one such occasion when he came to consult a lawyer on a legal issue, his only son *Kuanr Govinda Chandra* had accompanied him to Cuttack. Samanta took his son along with him whenever he visited places outside the village these days. The boy was his only child, the pupil of his eye. He could not afford to keep him out of his sight. *Govinda Chandra* was the lone progeny of his glorious *Srikarana* clan. He was the true image of his father, the luminous scion of his family. He was the glowing crescent moon in the sky of the *Srikarana* dynasty. How could his father keep away from him? But the lawyers, the deputy magistrates, and other clerical employees of the court had something else to say. "*Sa'nte*," they submitted respectfully, "your son is so handsome and intelligent-looking—you must put him in a school at Cuttack so that he can learn English. One who does not know English is not counted as a respectable person these days even if he possesses immense wealth and a recognizable social status. You are such a renowned landlord. You must deal with important officials on a daily basis. During your time you have somehow managed to handle matters in your way. But at the present time, your conservative and orthodox manners will be looked upon with disrespect and derogation. But be sure that the next generation of the zamindars cannot stand equal in any respect to the officers unless they have knowledge of English."

This made sense. The zamindar realized that one can not do away with learning English these days. English is the royal language, the language that all the high-ranking officers spoke in. How could these officers understand the problem of the common people unless it was relayed to them in their language? The lawyers and their assistants were stuffing their wallets only because they communicate with the officers in English.

Though the zamindar understood the indispensability of learning English, his heart bled when he thought of leaving the boy alone in town. After much deliberation, it was decided that the boy would stay in Cuttack in the house the zamindar had in *Sheikh Bazar*. The two boys, *Govinda Chandra* and *Sadananda* stayed in that house along with old *Sridhara Dasa* who came from the zamindar's palace in the village and lived in the house as the caretaker of the boys. The barber boy *Saita* was there to run errands. Another barber and a milkman came from the village to look after the routine domestic chores and other sundry jobs. A brahmin was employed to cook for them, completing the setup.

CHAPTER - 3

Lord *Govindajiu* was the ancestral tutelary deity of zamindar *Baishnaba Charana Pattnaik's* family. His wife, *Sa'antani Haripriya* had worshiped the Lord day and night and performed several religious rituals in the Lord's name praying for a son. Finally, the Lord granted her prayer and blessed the zamindar couple with a boy. Since the boy was a boon from Lord *Govindajiu*, the gratified couple named their son after him.

The boy was handsome as a prince and wore an intelligent look. He was *kuanr* or *prince Govinda Chandra* to the people employed in the zamindar's palace and the tenants of the estate.

Only two *Srikaran* families, one of which was Sa'antani *Harapriya's*, lived in village *Gopalpur.* The other family that shared the same homestead was that of *Dushasana*, a boy two years younger than *Harapriya*. His family was not as well-to-do as that of *Harapriya's*. But the two children were close friends. They went to the same village school, played together and shared their joys and sorrows with each other until *Harapriya* was ten. The restrictions imposed on a girl after she attained a certain age by the conservative society of those days forbade the free movement of *Haripriya* and she remained mostly confined to the indoors after this age. Soon she was given away in marriage to *Baishnaba Charana*

Patnaik. At the time of her send-off to her in-law's village, *Dushasana* came to meet her. *"Apa,"* he said with tear-filled eyes, "You will live the life of a queen now. You won't remember me. But who shall support me now in my time of need?"

But *sa'antani Haripriya* did not forget her childhood friend. After a few years, she found a suitable match for him and got him married. Since *Dushashan* was a poor boy, the *sa'antani* took care of all the expenses. But now, he had two stomachs to fill instead of one and without a regular source of income. The benevolent *sa'antani* took care of that too. Through the influence of her husband, she got *Dushasan* employed as a tenure holder of the *mouza Gobindpur* and brought his young bride to the palace. She was a bride of a *Srikaran* family after all. She should live like one. There were more than sixty maids in the ladies' wing of the palace to attend to different duties. The maids were all eager to wait upon *Dushashan*'s bride when the *sa'ntani* introduced her to them as her younger brother's wife. They addressed her as *sana sa'antani*. Alas, *Dushashan* proved to be a dishonest man. He not only ill-managed the affairs of the estate but siphoned a major chunk of the money that came as taxes to its treasury. Because he was an old acquaintance of his wife, the zamindar instead of terminating him forthright, got him employed in a ministerial job under the manager of the *mouza Dumdumpur*. But the nature of a man is not easy to change. After all, the bitterness of *Neem* fruit will never subside even if milk and sugar are regularly poured at the base of the tree. No sooner than he joined at his new post complaints against *Dushashan* reached the zamindar from *Dumdumpur*. He was up to his old tricks again and misappropriated the estate's money. It also came to the notice of the zamindar that *Dushashan* had collected tax-money from some of the villagers without giving them a receipt. But *Dushashan* did not live to reap the consequences of his wrongdoings. One morning the report from *Dumdumpur* reached the zamindar that *Dushashan* had succumbed to cholera. His only son was four years old at the time of his death. The kind *sa'antani*, her heart moved by pity for the fatherless child, came forward to take charge of the boy, *Sadananda*. Her own son, *Kuanr Govind Chandra* was only an infant of one year at that time. "My *Sadei* will always be my priority, my son comes next to him," the *sa'antani* said.

CHAPTER - 4
A DECADE PASSED

Nothing significant which requires special mention occurred during the first ten years the two boys lived in Cuttack, studying at the Queen's Mission School. Schooling completed, they went to college for further education. It was then that things slowly began to change. Until then, the expenses and other matters were managed by *Sridhara Dasa,* the old *Karana* who lived with them as a warden and caretaker. But now *Sadananda* decided to take over. The first change came in the form of the removal of old *Sridhar Dasa* from his duty. He brought the cash-safe into his own custody and took charge of keeping accounts of household expenses. He wrote a letter to *Sa'ante* zamindar *Baishnaba Charana* informing him about his decision. "Why to waste good money by appointing a person just to take the minor responsibility of managing the household expenses? I can take care of this," he wrote.

The zamindar *sa'ante* was glad when he read the letter. "The boys are getting worldly; good!" he said to himself. *Sadananda* always had the final say in all matters relating to household affairs. *Kuanr Govinda Chandra* did not want to bother himself with money matters. At the time of leaving the village, the *sa'antani* had advised *Sadananda* to look after the *kuanr.* "My dear son *Sadei,*" she had said, "now that you are going to live in a foreign place, both of you must take good care of your health. Always be by your younger brother's side and take care of him." The *sa'antani* knew that *Sadananda* was a clever boy and kept his eyes open to what went around. The *kuanr Govinda Chandra*, on the other hand, was simple and innocent. But he had one very special feature in his character. You might call it a vice or a virtue but once he made up his mind to do something, nobody could convince him against it. His mother had asked him to obey his elder brother. He trusted *Sadananda*. Nothing would change that.

Sridhara Dasa had run a smooth household. Now, his absence had upset the status quo. New problems came up almost every day. Some days there was no money to get the provisions from the market. Other days, there was a deliberate delay in the supply of groceries by regular suppliers. There were days on which the domestic help and other servants had to go without food. And there was a large amount due to the shop-keepers. But they did not mind supplying provisions on credit. The boys belonged to a wealthy landlord's family, they thought. They would surely make the payment one day or the other. It was not that there was no selfish interest involved in this generous behavior of the shopkeepers. They knew that no one would have time or interest to check or verify the rate of the goods. Taking advantage of the boys' wealth, they would ask for a price that was about four times more than the market price. The elder boy, *Sadananda*, was not so strict about keeping account of the expenses. At the same time, he spent lavishly on his friends, organizing parties from time to time. Because of this extravagance, there was often a shortage of money to meet regular household expenses.

Besides the amount due to different shops, *Sadananda*

had also incurred many other debts. He had borrowed a lot of money by simply giving out hand-notes. The barber *Saita* was greatly displeased with him for this irresponsible behavior. But he was aware of his position. After all, he was just a servant. It would be discourteous on his part to point it out to his master. Though a barber by caste he was clever and a loyal fellow. He revered his masters as God and would not hesitate to sacrifice his life for them if there was ever a need. For *Saita*, the *kuanr Govinda Chandra* was the real master. He always remained by his side like a shadow. The *kuanr* also liked him a lot. When the activities of the elder brother *Sadananda* became too much to bear, *Saita* tried to bring it to the notice of the *kuanr*. Several times he tried to broach the topic in an indirect manner. But the younger master reacted indifferently to it. *Saita* could not summon the courage to press the matter any further.

CHAPTER - 5
RAJIV LOCHAN

The zamindar of *taluk Samsharpur, Samanta Sankarshan Mahanty* was not an educated man. But he understood the worth of education. "Why else were the men of the *Srikaran* society of *taluk Dashagram* held in such high esteem? Why did they give themselves so much air? Did all of them have a pair of a horn on their heads?" He used to remark often. "It is because they know the value of education. All the men in that society whether rich or poor, are educated and most of them are in government jobs. There are no beggars there. The caste discriminations are often eclipsed by the prestige a man earns through the acquisition of knowledge. Honour dwells where wisdom, power and wealth lie. An educated man is always regarded with respect." The zamindar had, therefore, made a serious endeavor to educate the children of his own society. He took special care of educating children who belonged to poor families. He would provide them with food and clothing and bear all the expenses of their education. He had put up primary schools in many *Karan* villages of his estate.

He might not be modern in his thoughts, but he also understood that educating the girls would play an important role in the progress of society. Educated girls could keep account of household expenses. They could read the spiritual texts like The *Srimad Bhagabata* and other *Puranic* texts and recite them to the womenfolk of the village.

A primary school for girls was set up on the premises of the temple of Lord *Kunjabihari*, the tutelary deity of the village. At first, the *Karan samantas* were reluctant to allow their daughters to walk down the village street to attend school. When the zamindar's daughter *Indumati* was sent to school, they no longer had any objections. It was agreed that the girls would study in the school until the age of seven. Elder girls would not be sent to school. The classes were held in the afternoons. A *Paika* kept guard at the temple gate while the girls studied. No one was admitted inside while class was in session. The village school teacher, *Debibara Ojha* was around eighty years old. He was famous in villages near and far as a great teacher of mathematics. He had read *the Lilavati Sutra* thoroughly. The legend went that the old teacher, applying those formulae, could not only count the leaves on a Banyan tree but could also count the feathers of a bird in flight. Of course, there was no one educated enough to challenge or test the veracity of such claims. Teacher *Ojha* claimed that the zamindar *Sa'anta's* success in life was due to the discipline his cane had shown the zamindar. He proudly announced that more than half of the school teachers in the district of Cuttack were his students. He at present received a salary of two rupees a month. During the day time, he managed with *Prasad*. Besides the cash payment, he was also offered many gifts by the villagers. But the occasion of *Sri Panchami* was the heyday for him. It was on this day he earned more than he earned in a year otherwise, both in cash and in-kind.

Rajivlochan topped the list of the many boys whose education was financed by the zamindar. He was a bright student with a quick wit. He was a second-year in college in Cuttack. Not much was known about *Rajivlochan's* ancestry. His friends and fellow students in the college at Cuttack knew him as the zamindar's own nephew. His widowed mother *Tara Dei* had been living in the zamindar's palace for a long time, attending to household chores. Her position in the palace had been raised significantly after her son passed the Matriculation examination. It was said that the good or evil actions of sons bring their parents either fame or notoriety. *Rajivlochan's* achievements had promoted his mother's status in society. She no longer had to work hard, long hours. After the demise of the *sa'antani,* she looked after the important affairs within the inner wings of the palace. The servant maids of the palace now took orders from *Tara Dei.* Recently at the orders of the zamindar *sa'anta* himself, *Tara Dei* has supervised the affairs of the main wing as well. Strict as she was, if she reprimanded the servant maids for their misconduct, the disgruntled lot would whisper abuses on her when she could not eavesdrop, "Ohh! It was only yesterday she was pounding the husking pedal along with us. Now she goes about, bossing us around. It is because the good *sa'antani* has left for the heavenly abode that we are subject to such humiliation."

CHAPTER - 6
INDUMATI

Since the day *Sa'antani Lalita Dei* had left the world, the zamindar hardly showed any interest in the matters of the palace. *Tara Dei* had taken charge of its internal affairs. And in case there was a need for outside help, the watchman of the inner wing old *Madan Mahakuda* would carry a message to *Sachi Mahanty*, the *Karan* or the steward of the palace. News concerning minor issues of the palace never reached the ears of the zamindar. Only important matters were brought to his notice. The zamindar *sa'ante* paid a visit to the inner wings of the palace occasionally, to see his daughter *Indu*. *Marua*, *Indumati's* maid quickly rolled out a carpet on the verandah outside *Indumati's* bedroom. The *sa'ante* sat his daughter beside him and intoned his blessings fondly stroking her head. The girl had only recently lost her mother. Her father tried to assuage her grief diverting her mind to other matters. He told her about her rights over the enormous property he had earned hoping it would recompense her sense of loss to some degree. But the girl's large eyes brimmed with tears as she sat listening to her father's consoling words.

Indu was a playful, sprightly girl before her mother had passed away. Like a young doe, she bounded and sprinted about the palace joyfully. Her mother's death had changed her completely. She was no longer the *Indu* of earlier times. She had become as inert and expressionless as a heavy stone. She spoke very little nowadays, preferring to spend her time sitting alone, holding a book. But she was not reading. She just kept looking at the pages vacantly, her mind far away. Her mother, while alive, had engaged about ten servant maids to wait upon her daughter. Buy *Indu* did not speak to them. It was only *Marua* she trusted and disclosed her private thoughts to. *Marua*, too, attended to her with utmost sincerity. *Marua* was about seven years older than *Indumati* and was now in her prime youth. She was one of the many parentless girls the zamindar-palace had housed. Her conduct and bearing made one guess that she must have come from a decent family. She did not shout and scream like other maids. She never spoke harshly. She never laughed and giggled without a reason as the others did. She spoke softly, a sweet smile always on her lips. She always draped her head with a long-drawn veil that reached her eyebrows. She walked without making a sound. Her demeanor and her deportment, her good looks and well-proportioned figure were evidence enough to justify her noble birth. She, too, did not mix well with other maids, nor gossiped with them. She only loved to keep *Indumati's* company. *Marua* was always wherever *Indumati* was. Remaining in close companionship with the zamindar's daughter, Marua had learned to read and write. Sitting together in the solitude of her room *Indu* and *Marua* painted pictures of lotuses or those of Lord Krishna under the *Kadamba* tree. The relationship they shared always annoyed the other maids. "*Marua* is everything to her," they discussed sadly, "Why should we remain here when she does not need us? We might as well move out of the palace."

CHAPTER - 7
STUDENTS' ASSOCIATION

Some college students in Cuttack had formed a forum to discuss contemporary issues and other serious matters. It was held on the evenings of the first Saturday of every month. The educated youths had finally understood the importance of respecting one's mother tongue. They had realized that the progress of a community largely depends on the growth and prosperity of its language. Dr. Asutosh Mahany, vice-chancellor of Calcutta, a scholar, linguist and an authority on the *Sashtra*s, after experiencing this truth in his own life, has passed directives to include the study of vernacular in the course curricula of universities. He had observed that true wisdom could never be acquired through foreign languages. What is required is an analytical study of one's own mother tongue. The educated mass of our country has been drawn towards their mother tongue to a considerable extent. They have witnessed how the time-honored *Utkaliya* people, because of such a decline in its growth and rise had been subject to slights and slanders of the neighboring territories despite its splendorous antiquity. Our mother tongue basically does not have any repulsive attributes. Rather, it is more pleasing and has a more glorious past than many other languages. It is a prodigy with an illustrious ancientness and has a streak of humanness and decency about it. All those languages which before half a century or so shrank away from keeping proximity with our sacred mother tongue, are now looking down upon it with contempt. The bejeweled look these languages keep flaunting about is an adornment with the borrowed ornaments from the treasure-house of other illustrious languages of the world. Our own language, therefore, though naturally beautiful, feels inferior and shies away from them.

Noble natured sons, it is said, elevate the position of their mothers. Watching the respect, the *Pandava*-mother *Kunti* enjoyed even during the period of their exile, the *Kaurava* queen *Gandhari* might certainly have felt dejected. 'Misfortune wouldn't have befallen me had I have only one noble son like *Arjuna* instead of these one hundred useless ones!!" she must have thought.

The educated youth perhaps have realized in the meanwhile that the imperial language they revered might be rich and splendorous, and famous worldwide. But to hope that worship of that royal language could bring prosperity to the language of our own community is nothing but bitter irony. That language might be the venerable wish-granting goddess for our educated mass, but she is not genuine in her affection like the real mother. There might be instances of individual devotees of our own community attaining material success through her blessings. To believe that the worship of that language would fulfill the collective need of procuring eminence for our own mother tongue is only a mockery of expectation. The educated young men have also felt that even though hundreds and hundreds of years of austere worship of that goddess could not grant them the boon of mastery over the language. Our knowledge of that imperial language could not change the status of our community that has always been regarded as low and marginalized. We too, through our brief observation of the situation have come to realize that in any form of study, discussion or review made in a foreign language the knowledge remains confined only to those having proficiency in that language. Like a drop of ghee in water remains as it is in it, such discussions do not yield a result that is either expansive or extensive. On the other hand, such discussions in one's mother tongue evoke a widespread response like a drop of oil in water, spreading out in all directions.

To put an end to the humiliation our country was passing through a group of educated young men, who championed the cause of our mother tongue had shouldered the responsibility of wiping off the blot of ignominy stamped on its image. A parallel group of enthusiastic youth motivated by strong patriotic sentiments had taken a pledge to abandon all their individual materialistic interests and personal ambitions for the sake of their motherland. They were even ready to sacrifice their lives if the need arose. People of the older generation who professed their loyalty and love for their motherland but were incapacitated either by their advancing age or lack of strong will were delighted to watch the way these youth organizations functioned. They prayed for the long lives of these young men and lived with the hope of experiencing the joy of freedom before their end came. These kindred souls waited for that day as they prepared for the quietus without any fear.

In each session of the Forum for Discussion, the student members recited poems and prose articles written by them. The members greatly admired the rich emotional expressions and fine lyrical quality of *Kuanr Govinda*

Chandra's poems and agreed unanimously that he possessed an unparalleled talent. Some members did not hesitate to announce that he would be, in the near future, regarded, as a great poet. *Rajivalochan,* also a member of the forum, however, had a slightly different opinion in this regard. '*Kuanr Govinda Chandra* doubtlessly possesses rare poetic creativity,' he said. 'But I must be frank in my opinion. I must say that the poems of *Indu* if we consider the discrete choice of phraseology, prosody and above all the poetic spirit embedded in them, would prove as of much higher quality.'

Like a thin layer of cloud floating past the brilliant full moon, a film of gloom shadowed the smiling face of the *Kuanr* as he heard the remark. Anyone looking closely at him could have noticed it. The members, however, could not mark the change that came over the *Kuanr's* face, but it did not escape the probing eyes of *Rajivlochan.*

Some of the members instantly asked in one voice: 'Really? Who is this *Indu babu*? How do you know him?'

'No, no. It is not *Indu babu*. It is a *she*. *Indu* is my sister.'

'But the other evening you told that you had no siblings', *Ghanashyam babu* asked, surprised.

'Actually, she is the daughter of my maternal uncle, the only child of the zamindar of *Samsharpur.*'

'Did she go to school?' *Ghanashyam babu* inquired.

'No, she didn't. Uncle had engaged a couple of pundits to teach her different subjects at home. The girl is exceptionally intelligent. She is so proficient in all subjects, be it mathematics or literature. I am sure that no child of her age could stand a match to her. She could also paint pictures. But of course, she has not attained enough expertise in painting for lack of proper training.'

Ghanashyam babu looked expectantly at *Rajivlochan* for a long time. He wanted to know more about this

Indumati. But he could not gather the courage to ask any further questions. After all, the young woman who had roused his interest so greatly belonged to an aristocratic family. It would be against propriety to reveal his anxiety to learn more about her. Earlier it was considered improper and disgraceful to discuss the young female members of the family in any social gathering. But times have changed now. Western manners and morals have invaded the very core of our beings. These are the days of modern thinking. We are now witnessing the inception of a movement promoting women's education. Educated young men of these days relate happily with pride to their friends about the educated sisters and sisters-in-law in their family.

The discussions had centered around *Indumati. Kuanr Govinda Chandra* and his poetry were pushed to the background. The members were now greatly interested in *Indumati.* The very thought of a young girl who belonged to a conservative *Karan* family and lived in a village had acquired such knowledge that amazed them. On learning about *Indumati's* artistic skill they were assured that the darkness of ignorance that pervaded *Utkal* and where all social evils were bred would not take long to dissipate. *Rajivlochan* cast furtive glances at *Kuanr Govind Chandra* while the conversation was going on. A secret joy seemed to tickle *Rajivlochan* as he watched the look of despondency on the latter's face.

It was true, however, that none of the members had firsthand knowledge about *Indumati's* academic or poetic achievements. In fact, no one knew for sure if she could at all write poems. But their reverence for *Indumati's* poetry had reached such a height that there would perhaps have been a clash of opinions regarding whom to offer a seat first if the companion of goddess *Saraswati* and *Indumati* made their entry there at one time.

At the same time, it had occurred to some of the members to read *Indumati*'s poetry and examine its artistic quality. Such intolerance, however, is unbecoming of decent, educated young men. But the youthful enthusiasm usually triumphs over the prudence and patience acquired through learning and training. We, on our part too, have serious doubts about the poetic genius of *Indumati,* or the claim that she excelled *Govind Chandra* in poetry writing. We even doubt that *Indu* could at all write poems. It could rather be assumed judging the circumstances that the conflict between the two zamindar families resulting from the caste issue had prompted the envious *Rajivlochan* to concoct the tale of *Indumati's* poetic enterprise. Though *Rajivlochan* was in the same class as *Kuanr Govind Chandra* and *Sadananda* they were never been on friendly terms. Hardly there was an exchange of a word amongst them. *Rajivlochan's* face was often seen creasing with a suppressed malevolence as he watched *Govinda Chandra* reading poems or heard others praising him. It was obvious that people belonging to the *taluka Samsharpur* and people of *taluka Dashagram* nurture a natural hostility against one another. Like two kittens screaming at each other, a chance meeting between persons from each *taluka* invariably led to a noisy fight.

It is but obvious that individuals belonging to families of two warring clans would develop a natural antagonism against each other.

CHAPTER - 8
KUANR GOVINDA CHANDRA'S ANXIETY

Specific circumstances and a keen interest arousing from either good looks or admirable qualities of a person usually draw young men and women closer. Such enticement is sometimes referred to as love. Under the influence of this overwhelming passion, people experience a strange disquiet and restlessness. The irrepressible desire drives them to a state of uncontrollable anxiety. This anxiety, betraying all caution and care, finds its way to faces. People can try as much they might; they cannot prevent the disturbed state of mind expressing itself on their facial contour.

A distinct change had come over *Govinda Chandra* since he had learned about *Indumati's* special talent. People who were not close to him perhaps failed to notice it. But two people, *Govinda Chandra* himself and *Rajivlochan* could sense a change. While it filled the former with an anguished restlessness, it delighted the latter. It was the enmity between their families that prompted *Rajivlochan* to invent the episode, fictitious or true, of *Indumati's* excellence in poetry in order to spoil *Govind Chandra's* reputation as a good poet. In the meantime, *Rajivlochan's* hostility towards *Govind Chandra* had undergone a change as well. He was now sincerely trying to revive and improve his relationship with

the brothers. Recently the three of them *Rajivlochan,
Sadananda, Kuanr Govind Chandra* were seen strolling
together in the evenings, talking amiably to one another.
Rajivlochan, whenever he was alone with *Govind Chandra,*
never failed to make passing reference relating to *Indumati.*
Feigning he was doing it unintentionally, he often spoke
about her good morals, her beautiful look, her pious nature,
and decent manners. *Govind Chandra,* for his part, listened
to *Rajivlochan,* apparently disinterested, a faint flush flitting
across his young face.

CHAPTER - 9
SAITA'S MISGIVINGS

Saita was seriously worried. He too had noticed the changes in *Kuanr Govind Chandra.*

"What is the matter with the younger master?" he wondered. "He seems to have lost all interest in his studies. In the evenings he sits alone, plunged serious thought, with a blank look on his face. He doesn't even pay attention to what he eats anymore. Some days, he doesn't touch his food and other days, he gobbles it down in twenty seconds." As far as *Saita* knew, the younger master was not ill. *Saita* was puzzled. He knew that the younger master confided only in him and trusted him with all his secrets. He would have let him know if there was anything wrong with him. *Saita* could not decide what to do under such circumstances. He wondered if he should send a message to the zamindar-palace. But he dismissed the idea at once, "Who knows, a small issue blown out of proportion may lead to disastrous consequences. I may even be dismissed from service!" Although he was extremely curious to know the reason behind such abnormal behavior of his younger master, he could not find an opportunity nor gather enough courage to ask the master directly. He was sure that the young master was not sick, at least in the clinical sense. But he had no doubt that the matter was serious. Maybe it was to do with college and classes? Maybe not, he decided on second thought. He had discreetly brought the issue up to *Dinu babu*, the son of *Shyama Dhal sa'ante* of the village. He was in the same class as the young master and would have known if there had been an issue with college or his studies.

There was another strange development that confused the loyal servant. The two brothers who hardly parted from each other before were now spending time separately. As soon as the evening lamp was lit, the elder master would go out and would not return until late into the night. Making a clever excuse for going to the market to get groceries, *Saita* had once followed him. He was surprised to find his elder master in the company of *Rajivlochan*. He found them talking in hushed voices on an unfrequented spot under a Banyan tree on the bank of river *Kathjori*. *Saita* wondered why his master was spending time with a man who belonged to the enemy family. They were not in talking terms before. What had caused such an affinity? He also noticed that both brothers talked for hours after the elder master return home. It was not wise to keep such close company with the members of the enemy family. There might be trouble if the news reached the zamindar *sa'ante*. "What should I do now?" *Saita* thought undecidedly. "I would rather caution my younger master before things went out of hand, and before the zamindar *sa'ante* comes to know of this. But would that be wise? Who knows, the brothers might unite against me! No, no I will not do that. I should wait and see what happens. After all, aren't the fruits of patience always sweet?"

CHAPTER - 10
SUMMER HOLIDAYS

Summer vacation had begun. Schools and colleges were closed. Students from out of town were preparing to go to their respective villages. The chief *Chhamukaran* of village *Chandanpur, Bidyadhar Patnaik,* along with two palanquins and palanquin bearers, reached Cuttack in the early hours of the morning on the very day vacation began. *The zamindar and sa'antani* had asked him to leave Cuttack with the two brothers as soon as the college closed. *Sadananda,* however, was delaying the journey. Consequently, the return was rescheduled to the next day. *Saita* these days was keeping a close eye on the movements of the elder master *Sadananda.* That evening he discovered the elder master meeting *Rajivlochan* secretly under the same Banyan tree on the banks of river *Kathjori.* Hiding in the shadow, the curious *Saita* crept as close as he could to the two, trying to listen intently. But they talked in such small voices that he could not hear anything. Only when they took leave of each other could *Saita* hear a faint few fragments of what *Rajivlochan* said, "Well brother *Sadananda,* you must be careful. See that the matter is not disclosed. The slightest leak will upset everything. And do not be late to return. Make sure to get back here at least before a fortnight before college reopens." *Saita* was thoroughly confused. "What could be the purpose of such secret rendezvous," he wondered. "They are from two inimical families. Such was the degree of animosity between them that one would not flick a glance at the other's face. What had happened that *Rajivlochjan* addressed the elder master as brother?!"

CHAPTER - 11
AT THE PALACE

The day after the college closed for summer vacation, the palanquins reached the main entrance of the palace at *Chandanpur*. It was dusk and the zamindar *Samanta*, sitting in the small temple adjacent to Lord *Govinda jiu*'s main temple, chanted his daily evening prayers. As the two boys bowed respectfully at his feet, the zamindar raised his hand to bless them and gestured silently for them to go inside. The *Sa'antani*, on learning of their arrival, stood to wait at the doorway leading to the main palace. The boys bowed at her feet. "Get up my sons," she said in a voice suffused with affection. She raised *Sadananda* by his hand kissed his forehead. It was *Sadananda* whom the *Sa'antani* always gave prior attention lest he, thinking he was the son of poor parents, would feel ignored and hurt. Then she gathered *Kuanr Govinda Chandra* in her arms. Her mother's instinct immediately warned her that something was not right with the boy. His skin felt dry to her touch. She looked intently at her son's face and to her dismay found that it looked very pale. "Why, what is this? What is the matter with you *Govind*? Were you not well? Were you sick?" she asked in one breath and broke into a sob. As tears ran down her eyes, she kept wiping them with the end of her sari. Drawn by the sound of her sobbing, the maids came out to see what was happening. Failing to understand what was going on, they gaped at the boys and their mistress, their eyes round and unblinking like those of a wild cat. Watching all this *Sadananda* broke in, "Aunt, why are you so upset? He is fine. It is just that he was studying hard for the final examinations. That is why he looks a little drawn and pale," he said consolingly.

"Why do you have to take classes that demand so much hard work?" the *sa'antani* complained. 'Enough is enough. There is no need to study any further. You should not go to Cuttack any more."

"The final examination for this year is over," *Sadananda* said trying to soothe her. "The next examination will be next year. We do not have to study this hard then. We will just attend classes, get back home, eat and relax. We could also visit you time and again – whenever we find a chance. Don't you worry."

Sadananda's solicitations seemed to have convinced their disconsolate mother a little.

'Yes, yes, do that. *Sadei,* you know that *Govind* is not mature enough. Whenever you find the time you must come here along with him.' Satisfied, the *sa'antani* called out to the maids who had gone back inside, 'Hey, *Kanaka* and *Padi!* Get the water pot and the foot-mat. Quickly! Ask *Lalita Nani* to come to my quarters with cold drinking water and refreshments."

CHAPTER - 12
THE MARRIAGE PROPOSAL

"Have you noticed how *Govind*'s health has deteriorated? He always looks so pale and sick now!' The *sa'antani* told her husband in the seclusion of her bedroom as the couple sat on the bedstead. The zamindar listened to his wife but did not speak.

The *sa'antani* pressed on, "I asked *Saita* when he was alone if *Govind* was sick while at Cuttack, but he refused."

"*Sadei* says that *Govind* has lost weight because of the stress of exams. But I don't believe that. It's not like he hasn't taken exams before. He was stressed then too. But he has never looked so emaciated. And I noticed that *Saita* did not look me in the eyes as he answered my questions. He swallowed and fidgeted as if he wasn't being honest. I could tell he was hiding something from me. I interrogated him for a long time, but he wouldn't give up anything. I had to leave it at that as I realized that he wouldn't tell me even if he knew something. I have been watching *Govind* since the day he returned from Cuttack. He appears so withdrawn and remote. I find him sitting alone all the time, lost in thought. I am worried. Why don't you try to figure out what the matter is?"

"*Govinda Sri Hari, Govinda Sri Hari,*" the zamindar did not respond but continued chanting the names of God.

The *sa'antani* continued, "I think we should get him married sometime this year. I have an intuition that marriage will be the right solution. It would make him healthy again and mentally mature. And please be on the lookout for a suitable bride for *Sadei* too. Who else will do that for him other than us? We should even get them married at one time. That will be a big money saver," she added.

"*Govinda Sri Hari, Govinda Sri Hari*!! Let your wish be fulfilled O' lord," the zamindar finished his prayers and turning to his wife said, "All right. I'll see."

"What does 'will see' mean? Please take it seriously," the *sa'antani* sounded impatient. "Be on the job first thing in the morning tomorrow. Send for the *patjoshi*. Wait for an auspicious day and then send the mediators around in search of brides."

CHAPTER - 13
THE *KUANR* REFUSES TO MARRY

Could there be a dearth of aspiring parents for a son-in-law like the *kuanr Govinda Chandra*? He was the son of a landlord; no less than a king in his social status. The zamindar was the gem in the crown of the ilk of the *Srikaran*. He was a widely distinguished person, a man who enjoyed almost equal social privileges with the sahibs and government officers in high posts. And *Govind Chandra* was his only son, a young man as handsome as *Kartika*, the warrior son of Lord *Shiva*. Even a princess would have to have virtues earned through austere prayers and rituals to aspire for him as a husband. Once the news was out that the zamindar couple was on the lookout for a suitable bride for their son, stacks and stacks of birth-charts of prospective brides began arriving at the palace.

The zamindar *saa'nte* sat consulting privately with the old and experienced almanac-readers of the village, important *Karan* heads, and reliable priests and astrologers of his village. He had only kept a few birth-charts with him and returned the others to those who came carrying them. But he was quite hospitable and treated all the astrologers who came with the birth-charts respectfully. He saw to it that they were served good food and had a comfortable stay. As a parting gift, they were offered silk clothes and money for expenses for the journey back to their homes. He was agreeable and cordial in his behavior with them and did not reject any of the proposals. "Should the need arise I will ask for the birth-chart later," he assured them as he bade them an amicable goodbye. All of them with a feeling of assurance that the zamindar would consider the birth charts later. However, only two birth-charts, the daughter of *Ramaranjan Das Mandhata*, the zamindar of *Padmapur*, and the daughter of the zamindar of *taluk Saramara* were kept for further analysis. The solicitor-mediators of those households were yet to take leave of the landlord.

Sadananda was highly disturbed since he learned of these developments. He couldn't look *Rajivlochan* in the face if *Govind*'s marriage was materialized. But he could not dissuade his aunt or uncle from marriage plans. It would be disastrous if they had the slightest suspicion that he was playing the villain. No, that wouldn't do. He maintained a farce before people, trying to impress upon them that he was extremely happy about his brother's marriage. "Who knows about my marriage, what is the hurry? *Govind*'s marriage is much more important," he kept saying. "I must try to shoot the gun off *Govind*'s shoulder and try to stall the program," *Rajivlochan* thought inwardly. "Once I succeed in taking *Govind* back to Cuttack, I will set everything right."

It was the moth hour of the evening. A thick sheet of darkness was settling over the village. Smoke came swirling up from all the cattle-sheds of the village. The blowing of the conch through the village signaled evening worship in the temple. The maidens and brides of the village had long since collected water from the pools and went back to their homes.

Two young men, taking an unfrequented winding route through the mango grove on the western side of the river reached its bank. They sat down on the sturdy, twisted roots of the lone Banyan tree there, gazing at the water. For many years, the landmass on the western side of the river was slowly but interminably licked away by the river current. The soil under the old tree had partially slid off leaving half of its roots hanging in the air above the riverbed. In the flood seasons, the water in the river rose to touch these roots. However, since it was summertime, the river, except for a few small pools on its bed, was dry. The process of the drying of the river started from the winter month of *Pausha*. It was agreed that each family would have one pool at its disposal for collecting water; two pools for a large family. When the water dried up, everyone got together to dig the sand bed. When the bed was dug deep enough, crystal clear cool water would spring up, rising to a knee-high level. Even after the well was completely emptied it never went dry. In the next few minutes, it would fill itself up with water again. This was due to the ongoing undercurrent of water which kept the wells filled.

Sadananda looked up at the bank and saw a figure at a little distance standing there under the shadow of the large tree plastered in darkness. But *Sadananda* took a quick guess and called out," Hey *Saita,* go back to the palace and light the lamps in our study room. We will be returning in just a little bit." Without making a sound, the dark figure turned abruptly and walked back towards the village. "Well, well, playing hide and seek!!" he thought bitterly, "Let's see how long you will carry on the game!"

Sadananda spoke first, "*Govind*, the plan is being carried on in full swing. What do you think you should do now?"

"What plan brother? Are you speaking about my marriage?"

"Of course! What else?"

"My stand is clear and firm. I am not going to marry now!"

Sadanand felt relieved and happy at *Govind*'s reply. He knew *Govind* could be very stubborn at times. It was difficult to change or influence his decision once he made up his mind. This was one significant attribute in his character. He always believed his views and his decision to be perfect and granted them a priority. Probing further he said, "Don't say that. Won't it hurt uncle and aunt to hear you say things like that? You should judge things properly before taking a decision. Haven't you read *Bharavi?*'

Sahasa bidadheeta na kriyam abibakam paramapada padam Brunute hi bimarshya karinam gunalubdhah swayameba sampadah

One should not act without thinking. Impulsiveness always invites trouble. Those who reason properly before they act acquire the prize they aspire for.

"Every human being is a free and liberated creature. It would be foolishness on his part to act against his own judgment and conscience," Govind replied.

The two mediators who had brought the birth-charts of the daughter of the zamindar of *Padmapur* and the daughter of the landlord of *Saramara* still stayed in the palace eating free meals and were waiting for the final decision. But the zamindar *Baishnaba Charana Patnaik* was still undecided. "The boys are old enough," he thought. "It would not be right to go ahead with wedding plans without their inputs."

Old *Padan Patnaik* was the uncle of *zamindar Baishnaba Charan* related through kinship. By virtue of that relationship, he was the grandfather of *Govind*. That day at noontime the old man walked into the palace walking stick in hand. The two brothers were in their rooms studying. Clever *Sadananda* guessed the cause of his arrival and tapped *Govind*'s arm with a finger and gestured at their grandfather. Smiling broadly, he greeted the old man effusively. "Come on in, grandfather," he said and holding his grandfather by his arm and helping him onto a chair.

The three of them indulged in small talk, discussing college matters and life in Cuttack. *Padan Patnaik* may have been an orthodox man from an older generation, but he had enough ideas about propriety. He knew it wouldn't be decent to mention the marriages so abruptly. But the time had come to approach the subject. Clearing his throat a few times he asked, "What is it that *Baishanaba* is so seriously planning these days my dear boys?"

"What do you mean grandfather?" both men asked in one voice.

"Don't try to be clever with me boys. The entire village is talking about it. The mediators and solicitors keep coming and going and here you two are, feigning ignorance! How funny!!" He smirked knowingly.

Neither *Govind* nor *Sadanand* said a word.

"Well well well! So, you do not know. Let me tell you then. Both of you are going to marry soon. Two brides, sparkling like stars in the sky will make their entry in the palace. The sooner this auspicious occasion arrives, the better. I have become old and am on the brink of death. I want to see the marriages performed before my own eyes before I go. I want to enjoy the marriage feast and receive the gift of silk clothes. My days are numbered. Your weddings will be a big festival for the village and we are all anxiously looking forward to the day. Let me tell you in case you do not know. Messengers and mediators came from many villages with the birth-charts of several maidens. Two out of the lot have been selected. The zamindar seems to have his mind made upon these two. They are the daughters of the renowned zamindars of *taluka Padmapur* and *Saramara*. Both girls are beautiful beyond description. They are educated too. It is a royal match indeed! All arrangements will be made immediately after you give your consent. In this month of *Jyestha*, there are only three auspicious days for performing marriages. After Jyestha, there will not be any auspicious days for the next few months so the weddings will have to be held soon."

Sadananda was cunning. He knew the art of manipulating things to his own convenience without coming into the picture himself, like the lotus that grows in the mud but is never smeared with it. He signaled *Govind* to answer their grandfather.

"Things would have been different were we not in college," *Govind* explained. "But our education has taken us ten long years. Father has been spending bags of money every month on our education. And we only have a few months left to go. The final examination of F.A is in March. We may not study further than that but we cannot leave it halfway through. We have to get through the F.A examination."

"There you have it, grandfather. You are a wise and practical man. We learn lessons about life from you. But you must know now, why we are unwilling to marry. Marriage will just be a distraction. It will spoil all the hard work we have done all these years, like a tiny hole sinking a huge ship. Please just wait a few months. We will humbly submit to your will once the studies are completed," *Sadananda* added politely.

"Hey, *Sadanand*, don't you try to teach me about life!" the old man sneered. "I know that studying English is not complete without passing the *Faye-Faye* examination. We are not asking you to drop out of college in the middle of the session. But what is the harm in getting married? The brides will stay here in the palace. You will go ahead and finish your studies in Cuttack and complete the *Faye-Faye* examination."

"No, grandfather. It won't work. Times have changed. It won't be possible to get through the F.A examination once we're married," *Sadananda* returned with the assertion.

CHAPTER - 14
RETURN TO CUTTACK

Saita had become very watchful. His inquisitive gaze was constantly following the movements of his elder master *Sadanada*. He could instinctively guess that something was up. But despite serious probing, he could not figure out what. He knew his elder master was a shrewd character. It would not be unusual if he created some trouble for his connivance. He was determined not to let any trouble befall his younger master, *Govind Chandra*. He noticed that the post peon was delivering post on alternate days for the elder and the younger masters. He also noticed, to his surprise, messengers from *taluka Samsharpur* in the village. Instead of coming directly to the palace, however, they waited in the mango grove on the west side of the village. In order to avoid run-ins with any village people, the elder master snuck out to the groves to collect messages in the semi-darkness of dusk. Sometimes he handed the messengers letters of reply too. *Saita*, keeping his presence unnoticed, had observed these interactions. He had seen the elder master tearing up some letters after going through them. He had managed to scrape together a few and brought them back to the palace and for the younger master to read.

That day, at noon, the post peon came to the palace carrying a long envelope. It was a registered letter, written in English. Both young masters were sitting together in the front yard. The elder one took the letter from the postman and without opening it, handed it to the younger master. *Govind Chandra* opened the letter and ran his eyes over its contents. "What is it?" *Sadananda* asked. The *kuanr* read the letter aloud:

Sri Sadananda Patnaik, Kuanr Govind Chandra Patnaik, Students of the Cuttack College of Arts, second year:

This is to notify you that the results of the final examination of your class will be released on the 2nd of June, Monday. You are required to be in attendance on the mentioned date.

Sd/ W. Jones
Principal, Cuttack College

The news spread through the palace in no time. "The big sahib has sent a summon. Both the sa'antas will have to go to Cuttack to pass the English examination." Soon enough, it was the talk of the village.

The boys went to the zamindar with the letter. *Sadananda* handed it to the zamindar *Baishnaba Charan Patnaik* and explained its contents. The zamindar *sa'anta* turned the envelope back to front on his palm a few times. "*Govinda, Govinda, Sri Hari, Sri Hari* Let things happen as you wish them to!" he muttered and returned it to *Sadananda*.

The news had reached *sa'antani* by the time the boys entered her quarters in the inner section of the palace. She sat in her room silently, her cheek resting on her palm, looking heartbroken. "*Sadei* my child, didn't you tell me that the college will remain closed for two months and twenty days? I have been counting, and there are still seventeen days left. Then why this letter has been sent—?'

"Yes aunt, I had thought it would. But this is an official matter. Official directions must not be disobeyed," *Sadananda* tried to explain.

"You have studied enough English. What is the need for further studies? Don't you go to Cuttack again."

"With all due respect, that it will not be wise. We have spent ten long years studying in Cuttack. Now it is just a matter of a few months. Won't it be foolish to let all our labor go waste by dropping out at this juncture?" *Sadananda* tried to sound convincing. The *sa'antani* did not counter. But her eyes brimmed with tears. Silently she wiped them off with the end of her sari.

In order to be in Cuttack on Monday, the boys would have to leave on Sunday. The preparations for the journey had begun on Saturday. On Saturday morning the *sa'antani* sat still and wordless in her room, oblivious to her daily routine. Maid *Sankri* stood at the door with the bowl of oil, a bath towel, and a silk sari. The *sa'ntaani* took no notice of her. "Madam," the maid ventured with folded hands, "It is long past your bathing time. The morning worship of the deities is also getting delayed."

The *sa'ntani*, unable to control her worries, sent for her husband.

"I don't have the heart to send the boys back to Cuttack. I don't know why but I have an intuition that something isn't right. Couldn't you go with them to make sure that they are safe and sound?" she said persuasively. The zamindar was a somewhat dispassionate character. He did not involve himself much in such matters. He had firm faith in lord *Govindjiu* and believed that everything happened according to His wish. That all efforts of man to accomplish anything go in vain unless the Lord willed it. That man has no control over anything nor the power to change it. But he did not discuss or debate with his wife and left uttering the name of the lord. The *sa'antani*, aware, of her husband's nature, did not want to stretch the subject.

All arrangements for the journey were completed by the early Sunday morning. *Saita* had taken care of everything. He was a competent fellow and was never in need of any push to get a job done. As the boys touched their mother's feet to their heads and bade her farewell, the *Sa'antani*, pressing her lower lip hard with her upper jaw tried desperately to control the sobs that rose inside her. She knew that weeping during the ritual of *dahi machha* was inauspicious. But it was too much of an effort to hold the obstinate tears in check. She embraced *Sadananda* tears streaming down her eyes and said, "Come, my child, come to the temple of *lord Govindajiu* to get his blessings. You must have a few drops of the holy water with which the Lord's feet were washed. Then start your journey by putting the garland of holy basil that was taken off the deity around your neck. *Sadei* my son, please take good care of your younger brother *Govind*. He has not matured enough to look after himself. Both of you must take your food on time and go to bed on time. Do not exert yourselves and never go out at night."

She accompanied the boys to the temple, pressing the border of her sari to her eyes, "Come dears, may lord *Govindaji* look after you." She said as she stood at the entranceway to see the boys off.

Since the journey was planned so suddenly, it had escaped everyone's mind to make sure they had started out on an auspicious day. On Sunday morning the chief astrologer walked hurriedly into the palace, his walking stick in one hand and a bundle of almanacs tucked under his arm. The two young men had already climbed into the palanquin by the time he had reached them. The chief astrologer, without a word, sat down in one corner of the porch of the cutchery hall, leaning on its fencing. After the palanquins moved away the zamindar's eyes fell on him.

"Ohh! How forgetful of us! It did not strike us to send you a message. But now that you have come, find out if today is a favorable day for the journey."

The chief astrologer simply said, "Yes, sir."

The zamindar *sa'anta* noticed that the face of the astrologer had paled, and he sat silent and still as a log of wood.

"Look it up in the almanac and find out!" the *sa'anta* persisted.

The astrologer took out a piece of chalk from his waist fold and drew *kuanr Govind Chandra* 's horoscope on the floor. He had memorized the planetary positions in everyone's horoscope in the zamindar family. He wrote down a few digits below it and sat quietly fixing his eyes on the pages of the almanacs.

"What, what is it?" the zamindar inquired.

"Sir..."

"The young masters have left. You can tell me what you noticed."

The *patjoshi* took a deep breath and said, "Today the *Ashlesha naxatra* will remain in the zodiac for about twenty-six minutes and fifteen or so seconds. Then *Magha* will move in to replace it. This period of transition is not favorable for any auspicious undertaking since it marks the beginning of a bad time. Cuttack lies in the north direction which today is guarded by the sinister *yogini*. In addition, today, the moon enters the sign of Sagittarius which will cast an evil influence on the *kuanr's* horoscope since his moon sign is Taurus and the moon in his horoscope is in the eighth house. Even the time of sunrise today is not favorable for taking a journey— a number of bad omens!!" the *patjoshi* sounded gloomy.

"Govinda Govinda! Sri Hari Sri Hari! As you wish!" the zamindar Sa'anta said.

"'But the educated mass of these days do not believe in these predictions. What about that?" the *chhamukarana* said in a lighter tone.

The old midwife *Kaushuli* who had come to watch the send-off rituals of the two young masters stood there in a corner, listening to the conversation. Hearing the astrologer's predictions, she hurried into the inner quarters and reported to the *sa'antani* about what she has heard. The *sa'antani*, overwhelmed with fear, quickly opened her trunk and took a hundred and eight rupees out. She touched the money to her forehead and sent it to the zamindar with orders to perform necessary precautionary worship in order to appease the hostile planets.

Upon the advice of the principal astrologer, seven learned Brahmins were elected to offer worship to different deities. They would chant a thousand names of Lord Vishnu and Goddess Durga and recite the *Chandi Patha*. They were also to perform the ritual of placing one hundred thousand pitchers at the temple of Lord Shiva and offering one lakh basil leaves at the feet of lord *Govindajiu*. The principal astrologer perused meticulously over the horoscope of the zamindar's son, made his calculations and reached the conclusion that the *kuanr* was under the strong influence of planet *Shani*. This planet dreaded as a trouble-maker cast its evil spell on the boy's horoscope. One relieving factor, however, was that the planet was likely to spell danger to the life of a spouse. Since the *kuanr* was not married there was no fear on that account. It was unanimously decided that a *Graha Bhattarika* ritual or *yajna* was to be performed to please the deities residing in all the planets. It was decided that the list of ingredients for the ritual and method of observing the worship was to be sorted out the next day. The reputed priest of the village, *Trilochana Mahapatra Tihadi* notified the *zamindar* that the original text containing the list of the ingredients required for the *yajna* and the method of worship was with him. "It was taken down from the old almanac by my father's elder brother. The list and methods were written in his own hand. Whenever such a *yajna* is performed in our village or the villages nearby, messengers from those families would come to copy down the methods of observance and the list from this handwritten text."

CHAPTER - 15
THE ESTABLISHMENT IN CUTTACK

The environment in the house in Cuttack had changed distinctively. *Saita* could sense it soon after their arrival. Before summer vacation, the establishment was run on the borrowings from different sources. Lack of funds had led them to procure provisions from different shopkeepers on loan. Now, there seemed to be an endless source of cash. *Saita* had recently seen the elder master tying up several notes in a bundle. He had been quick to hide the bundle, noticing *Saita's* gaze upon him. "Where had all that cash come from all of a sudden?" *Saita* wondered. As far as *Saita* knew, the elder master never made a budget nor maintained an account book. His extravagance had reached its peak. He observed that the elder master was buying things at the initial price shopkeepers quoted without caring to bargain. The cunning tradesmen of Cuttack must have been making quite a profit out of his carefree manner.

"I have seen with my own eyes the cashier of the palace give a hundred and fifty rupees to the elder master for household expenses at Cuttack. The entire amount was exhausted in paying the shopkeeper *Sauri Sahu*. How is the cashbox still loaded with money?" *Saita* thought to himself. He could not solve the riddle despite applying all his wit. His suspicions grew when he realized that all sorts of money transactions were made by the elder master, but only during the absence of the younger master. He decided not to poke his nose into the affairs of the masters. Why should he interfere? He was just a servant after all. After all, should a member of the bridegroom's wedding party interfere in the proceedings of the ceremony?

Saita had also noticed a big improvement in *Rajivlochan babu*'s financial condition. Last time he had seen the man, he was seeking shelter in the rooms of his friends' houses as he could not pay boarding fees to the university. But now he was renting out a two-story house near the university. A night-feast was organized just a couple of days after the masters had arrived at Cuttack. The young masters had rushed to Cuttack because they would pass the examination. Pass the examination—? What examination?! They did not seem to bother about the results of the college examination. Only parties and feasts —! A lot of whisperings and the jingling of coins! Let them do whatever they want, *Saita* thought resignedly, I am only concerned with taking good care of my younger master.

In the evening the elder master called the cook and asked him not to prepare food for both the masters' "Only cook for yourselves tonight. We are invited to a feast in *Rajiv babu*'s place."

"Come what may, tonight I must go there unnoticed and find out what is going on!" *Saita* told himself determinedly.

As both the masters set off to attend the feast the elder master called out to *Saita* and said, "We will return late. There is a large amount of money in the house and Cuttack is a dangerous place. So be watchful and never step out of the house. Do you understand?"

Saita took a deep breath before he replied, "Yes sir, I have understood everything."

"What do you mean by '*I have understood everything?!*'" the elder master demanded.

"I mean, master, I have understood all the instructions you have given."

CHAPTER - 16
THE FEAST

In a lane leading off the main road to Buxi Bazar there stood a two-storied building. The house was positioned lengthwise in a north-south direction. On the ground floor, a long, spacious verandah that led to a couple of rooms on its inner side ran along the entire length of the house. At the west end of the verandah, a staircase went up to the upper floor. The structure and design of the upper floor were identical to that of the ground floor. Two rooms of almost equal measurement opened to a long spacious, enclosed terrace that ran parallel above the verandah on the ground floor. Three large windows fitted with panels of stained glass let in enough light and air to keep the place well lit and ventilated. There was a rectangular compound leading off the verandah on the ground floor surrounded by brick-built boundary walls on three sides. Just in the middle of the boundary wall in the front, there was a big double-door gate that opened to the street. From this gate, a narrow pathway lined up on both sides with clumps of white jasmines went up to the base of the front verandah. The jasmine shrubs were planted in rows, each a cubit away from the other, maintaining uniformity of distance and a neat pattern. A pair of lotus-shaped ornate flowerpots stood at each end of the verandah where flowering creepers heavily laden with bunches of flowers swayed gracefully at the touch of a soft breeze. In the backyard of the house, a couple of tiled rooms stood against one side of the compound. One of these was used as a kitchen and the other served as a storeroom. A few yards away lay a well with circular fencing.

Hardeblal Bhagat was the owner of this house. His son, Ramdeblal Bhagat, a man with exquisite taste, had this house designed by an experienced architect for his own use. But now he had it up for rent. A month or so ago, a few young men, college students, had taken the house on rent. They used it as a mess and engaged a cook, a barber, and a couple of domestic helps to manage the establishment. These young men who belonged to the *taluk* of *Samsharpur* were rural characters and were guided by the instructions of *Rajivlochan*. *Rajivlochan* had warned them not to come out of the house or talk to an outsider. "If he finds anyone of you alone, the British contractor would take you away and sell you to the owner of the tea-estate to work as a slave," he had said. The gate at the front entrance was, therefore, always kept locked. *Rajivlochan* kept the keys with him.

For the past ten days, a feast was organized by the inmates of this house on every alternate evening. On these days, only two young men came to attend the feast. There were no other outside invitees. A meeting was convened on the first-floor terrace before the feast. A carpet was spread out on the floor where stood a big oval-shaped table covered with a large milk-white table-cloth. Seven straight-backed chairs were placed around the table. From a hook in the ceiling hung a chandelier (manufactured by Oslar Company) with seven branches with ornamental lamp-holders. Beautiful candelabrums were clamped to the walls. The place was brilliantly lit to give the impression of broad daylight.

On the first evening, *Kamala Lochan babu* addressed the gathering, "Esteemed members of the Association! It is true that an association without a president is as unthinkable as a kingdom without a king. All of you understand that in civilized countries like England, in every association where serious intellectual discussions take place, a president is formally elected to preside over the meetings. Last week, you must have read in the newspapers that His Excellency the Governor of Calcutta had chaired the meeting convened on the feast organized at Saint Andrews College. Here is an assemblage not commonplace or ordinary. All the members of this association are learned, independent-minded, not influenced by any social evil, and are from aristocratic backgrounds. A president is an absolute necessity for an assembly of such dignified members. I, therefore, propose here to elect *Samant kuanr Govind Chandra* as the president of our association. In my view, he is competent in all aspects to hold the office." All other members approved of the suggestion with loud applause.

Lambodar Dasa, another member, stood up.

"Um—um, President and the members of our association," — He abruptly stopped realizing that the president must be formally elected. "Um- um not now," he corrected himself with his habitual mumbling. "Um—um, I second this proposal," he said. *Babu Mukundaram Mahanty* also stood up. "I support it," he declared. All the members clapped loudly in approval of the proposition. *Govind Chandra* was had officially been elected as the president of the association.

Rajivlochan babu respectfully led the newly elected

president to his seat, a cushioned chair of teakwood covered with a velvet spread on which floral patterns were embroidered in golden and silver threads and sat him down. The president rose back to his feet and greeted the assembly. "Let the meeting of this evening begin with the accomplished speaker *Kamallochan babu* reading us one of his articles," he said. *Kamallochan*, as if he was ready long before for this, stood up with his paper in hand, even before the president had stopped speaking. He cleared his throat a few times before he spoke,

"Respected President, and the members of the Association! Our president has kindly entrusted me with the difficult duty of delivering a speech today. I know that even the thought of addressing an erudite assemblage such as this will be nothing but futile. But as an insignificant person, as I am, it is my humble duty to obey the president's order. I, therefore, will read out an article in this meeting. The subject discussed in the article is a serious one and relates to a basic issue of life for every man and woman. In a gathering like this, where everyone is an intellectual committed to the cause of our nation and wants the abolition of social evils, to speak on any ordinary or irrelevant topic will be a pointless effort. The title of the essay I shall be presenting is 'Choosing a Life-partner.'

"My dear friends! You are all well-read in the ancient scriptures of our country as well as those of the west. You too possess knowledge of the principles of philosophy. Darwin, the famous western philosopher, and biologist have expressed his views advocating the relevance of the subject with substantive and irrefutable evidence. I presume all of you know it. For promoting the growth and preservation of the animal kingdom, nature has prescribed certain laws pertaining to the sexual union of the animals as well as human beings. The violation of the law will lead the world to its doom. The Hindu scriptures often offer, as they do on many subjects, misleading and illogical views in this area. The views of the savants of the west in this context appear rather more sensible and acceptable. The brilliance of their wisdom has revealed new paths to approach the issue."

There was loud applause.

"We find ourselves astounded when we observe the inexorability of the force that impels even the lesser animals to participate in the act, let alone the rational human beings. It compels us to acknowledge and honor the mysterious schemes of nature and the profound influence it exercises on human beings and animals."

He paused for the applause to die down.

"You must not forget or ignore the fundamental fact that since the union of the opposite sex is an act decreed by Nature, both the male and female are guided by their own individual choice and discretion while participating in it. Sexual union is not a sin. In fact, there is nothing about the male-female union which could be defined as sin. In fact, the transgression of the law of nature is sin and this must never go unpunished."

"Before concluding this discourse, I would like to dwell upon some important points relating to the moral law that guides society while indulging in the act. And the possible consequences if such a relationship is influenced by perverse instincts.

A close study of human behavior introduces us to different types of individuals that exist in a society. While one segment follows exclusively a crude law of nature that applies to all animals, the other is an educated, civilized mass that is more refined, conscientious and is guided by healthy ethical and social norms. And then there is a third category comprising of conceited and prejudiced characters with a great degree of self-esteem. These individuals claim certain misleading notions as scriptural prescriptions and present them to be ultimate and authentic. These blind convictions eventually lead to a disastrous consequence. With a heavy heart, I must admit here that we, Hindus, belong to this last category."

There was more clapping.

"Amongst the many rules and regulations prescribed to sustain and support the human society, 'selecting a partner in sex' is considered as a top priority because a healthy sexual relationship guarantees lasting peace and happiness in the life of an individual. A right selection in this regard plays a significant role in the development of society while a wrong choice could be responsible for the decline of human society in general.

There are people who live in the lap of nature far from the reach of civilization. They follow a custom of their own when making a choice of their respective partners. I would briefly like to explain how the selection of a partner is made in the tribes of the *bhuyan*, *kandha* and the *dongra*. A marriage obtains the social recognition once a *dhaangra* puts a vermilion spot on the forehead of a *dhangri* and is celebrated with festivity and merrymaking. The whole community indulges in drinking, feasting, and dancing.

And of course, you all know very well, the healthy custom the civilized countries of the European continent especially France and Germany follow in choosing a spouse.

I seek your permission here to enumerate in a few words the conventional practices the Hindu society adopts in institutionalizing a marriage. You know that a large percentage of the Hindu population is poorly educated.

Obviously, the lack of clarity in understanding things in their proper perspective has led to distortion and abuse of a custom approved by minds enlightened with education. I would like to elaborate upon it. In order to assess the character of a community or class, it is necessary to study the character of the people in the uppermost level of that class – since the people at the lower segment in a society tend to imitate the conduct of their superiors. As all the members in this assemblage are from the *Srikkaran* society, we can easily form an idea about the general custom that is practiced in Utkal for executing a marriage once we try to examine the way marriages are institutionalized in our *Karan* caste.

The conjugal relationship once established and sanctioned a social recognition, becomes immutable and constant. The joy or sorrow resulting from the actions of either spouse must be a mutual experience. It is an unbreakable bond and both man and wife must bear through it for the rest of their lives whether they like it or not. The Christian and Islamic laws of marriage allow the disgruntled spouse the privilege of obtaining a legal or official separation. But our custom forbids us to avail such a privilege for escaping the trauma of an undesirable relationship.

My dear brothers! What should be our course of action in such a difficult situation? Such an orthodox custom is like an incurable disease. Is it not wise, therefore, to take preventive measures against an ailment which is incurable?"

There was loud applause at that.

"What I mean to say that if a wife – you may define her as the man's better half or his lifelong companion – unfortunately happens to be unlettered or a shrew or harsh or bereft of the feminine grace, she is to be abandoned in all circumstances. Before choosing a life partner, therefore, one must inquire into all these aspects and make a careful decision. I will cite one instance here to prove my point. How careful we are in selecting a pair of shoes for our feet! And that is for temporary use! Shoes are worn away in time and are discarded and replaced by a new pair. But a wife will remain with us all throughout our lives. Do we take even as much interest in selecting her as we take while selecting a pair of shoes for our feet? Instead of acting like an educated and judicious person, we just blindly follow an orthodox custom. I leave it to you to give it a thought and decide if such an approach is wise.

Let us now examine the procedures that are customarily followed by our society in negotiating a match. The ones that do not have the liberty to select a spouse of their own choice are destined to go through the aftereffects of it, bitter or sweet. As per the local custom, the responsibility of choosing a bride rests on either the elders of the family or their friends and relatives. It could not be refuted however that our elders and guardians will always think in terms of our good. They would never want their sons to marry the wrong candidate. But are the procedures they usually adapt to choosing the right candidate just or sensible? Do they get an adequate opportunity to judge the bride – her nature and her appearance? In our society of the *Srikaranas*, the father of the groom-to-be attaches priority to her caste if she comes from an aristocratic Srikaran family. He also makes an inquiry to find out with which other such Srikaran families they have been maintaining matrimonial relationships. Fifty percent of the job of bride-selection is done once it is proved that the bride-to-be's family too is pure, unalloyed *Srikaran*."

There was laughter at his words.

"Then there appears on the scene the astrologer, a stupid cheat of a man who claims himself to be a clairvoyant and demands a meager fee of a seer of rice and two *annas* for the day's hard work of making astrological predictions. He will peruse over the horoscopes, and after a little deliberation will declare that they match in eight respects. The horoscopes of the prospective bride and the groom never match in all nine respects, he would say emphatically. 'That would not be a problem. This fault could be easily remedied by offering some gold to the Brahmin who performs the marriage rituals and some money to the astrologer,' He would add. The preliminary responsibilities of matchmaking are discharged with this. And imagine who is entrusted with the job of inquiring about the looks and qualities of the bride-to-be? Always either domestic help or a village woman who does the job of pounding the husking pedal. The clever mother of the girl could bribe these women to describe her daughter as one of the best. She would be described to the groom's family as a maiden with a complexion of the champak flower, a nose as sharp as the edge of the sword-blade, well-read in classic texts, sings well and what not!!

'Friends! You have read many sublime tales of romance in the poems, plays, and novels. Would you expect to enjoy even a grain of that blissful conjugal love from such an erratic match? Why should the educated mass of the twentieth-century unthinkingly follow the laws of a faulty system like a sheep in a flock blindly following the one moving ahead of it and meeting with an accident as the inevitable consequence? Only the uneducated and the naive would do that. The case is different with the educated youth. They would evaluate things with a mind enlightened with knowledge. Armed with a judiciousness obtained through education they defy the evils prevailing in the society and pave the way to a trouble-free and happy life not for just themselves but for the oncoming generations too.

Friends, we must aim at the wellbeing of our 'holier than heaven' motherland and our own happiness by amending the age-old evil practices existing in our society. It's high time we channelized our efforts in this direction. The knowledge we have obtained through the hard work of studying so many books will be reduced to an absurd and meaningless waste unless we do that."

He paused again for applause.

"Because of the social evils and our blind adherence to a faulty custom, our Utkali community is deemed inferior and low when compared to other civilized communities. Hence, Dear friends! It is now the duty of every educated and conscientious individual to put in a determined effort to abolish social evils and promote sensible thinking. Doubtlessly, the task is not an easy one. But easy ways are for ordinary people. It is the bold and the brave that venture to choose the difficult path. A social evil is as harmful to individuals and to the society as contaminated blood running through our veins. How does patient suffering this ailment of blood-impurity react to the doctor who treats him? Certainly not in a positive or reciprocating manner! The social reformers, therefore, must face a lot of opposition and hostility at the initial stage, though, in later times they are assigned a deified status. As we set out on this noble mission, we must encounter several impediments in the beginning, but we must remember that these obstructions will not be there permanently. The passenger onboard is frightened out of his wit when a patch of dark cloud pregnant with thunder and lightning moves towards the airplane. A heart throbbing with fear imagines that at any moment, the turbulence will break the airplane into pieces. But miraculously, the very wind that has pulled the cloud patch towards the airplane blows it away in another direction.

Dear Friends! We must never fear the turbulence that may come in our way of accomplishing our purpose nor shall we ever be guided by selfish motives. Let the knowledge we have gleaned through education be used to better society. Friends, there are several important duties that demand our attention. The first and foremost of them is the right selection of a spouse since our life and its peace and happiness depend solely on our right choice of a life-partner. Let our discretion and judiciousness set an example for others. We should abide by the following three principles while choosing our would-be bride.

Number one, we shall not acknowledge any sub-categorization of our *Karan* caste. There should be no primary or secondary or lesser groups of *Karan*. We must treat all categories of *Karana* as equals.

Number two, it is a rare possibility to get a bride who is a poet. It takes several lives of austerity to attain one. But we must decide now that we will never marry an ignorant, uneducated girl.

Number three, it is, however, a little difficult to find an educated girl. Therefore, we will only pick a bride from villages where there are schools for girls.

Brothers! Please raise your hands if you approve of and accept the three principles I have mentioned."

Everyone in the room had their hands raised.

"Brothers! In the end, I request these principles be officially recorded in our register along with the signatures of all our members."

The applause signaled the end of the meeting.

CHAPTER - 17
THE CONSPIRACY

North of the city of Cuttack, there stood a dilapidated fort on a vast stretch of land, which presently goes by the name of *Killa Maidan*. The spot, believed to have held the memoirs of Utkal's freedom fight, bears quite a historical significance. Along the riverside, adjacent to its northern limits, a narrow road went arcing about the remnants of the once-massive fort. Almost touching its bounds and below the level of the road, there was a moat that circled the fort premises. Here, at this edge of the field, the river-bank was particularly lonely. A slim stream of clear water forked out from the main river flowing along this edge. There were years when it went rippling alongside the bank, and in others, it moved farther to the middle of the sand bed and flowed producing a sweet lapping sound. This portion of the river mostly remained dry during the summer. But in the rainy season, the river swelled with floodwater. The boats from Sambalpur and the western Gadjat provinces loaded with merchandise moored at the jetty were not spared from the furies of the storm and flood. They stacked up with goods to the edge of their uppermost borders and touching the slanting thatches over them were precariously exposed to the assaults of the stormy wind. Had it not been for the thatches, the cargo would have been drenched in the splashing rain. Fifty years ago, these cargo boats sailed across the *Naraz* deep and on entering river *Kathjuri* anchored at the jetty on the north side of the river. The boats no longer coursed that way after the barrage was built at *Naraz*.

It was sunset.

On that lonely river bank at the north of the *Killa Maidan* two young men, one about twenty-two years of age, and the other somewhere between nineteen and twenty sat looking at the streamlet.

The younger one was the first to speak. "I am so confused brother *Sadei*," he said uncertainly. "I can't decide. What do you think I should do?"

"This is what keeps troubling me day and night. For the last week or so I have been passing sleepless nights. You know you are everything to me. Whatever is good for you is good for me too," Sadanada replied. "But we must be very careful while planning our course of action. Priority should be given to the duty of reforming our society and progressing our nation. What is the use of acquiring knowledge if we let ourselves misled by blind convictions preached and propagated by a bunch of ignorant uneducated people? It will only pose a serious setback in the way of our country's progress. Be sure of that."

"It will be impossible to get brother *Rajivlochan*'s proposition materialized," *Kuanr Govindchandra* said. "Aren't we *Srikaran* by caste? They may be *Karan* by caste, but of a lower category. Besides, both families have been involved in several legal disputes for years. I don't believe father will give his consent to the match. However, let's presume that the father somehow is convinced. Will our kinsmen agree? Will they ever let the father establish a matrimonial relationship with an enemy family? And will a father ignore his kinsmen? I don't believe that. Do you?"

"Aren't you being a little orthodox and old fashioned?" *Sadananda* returned with slight reproach. "Times are changing and so are these conventions and the idiosyncrasies. I can even visualize the future. You must reshape your thinking accordingly, to match the changing times. You will have to prove yourself an ideal character by doing something exemplary. How could you advocate in favor of a vainglorious and reprehensible caste distinction? You are a higher-class *Karan* and *Rajiva* is one from the lower category of the same caste. How could you measure the degree of the aristocracy of both categories; and by what yardstick? How could you think of such a divisive issue at a time that when the preaching of the doctrine of universal brotherhood is the need of the time? Caste distinction is itself a divisive factor that deteriorates the progress of this nation. Further subdivisions of it will accelerate the process. Wisdom, wealth and a prejudice-free mindset are important for the growth and rise of a nation. The distinction between man and man is something unnatural. Such a distinction that amounts to a violation of natural law is liable to be punished. Haven't we read in the *Karma Yoga* section of the sacred *Srimad Bhagavad Gita* that it is the deed and conduct and not the caste that determines an individual's class? All *karana*s are equal in their thought and action, and in their conduct and bearing. What is the need then for putting them in separate categories? It is unnatural. Besides, both families are spending a huge amount of money in lawsuits. Instead of yielding any results, the legal issues are forcing innocent people to give false evidence. Quite a few villagers from either side were sent to prison because of that. Isn't it imperative on the part of an educated, prudent and compassionate person like you to take steps in this regard in order to prevent the families from indulging in an act that will sweep their treasuries clean? Isn't your responsibility to save the people that are compelled to commit the sinful act of testifying against the truth, and bring peace in the lives of the poor subjects who endure a hard time on no fault of their own? Your noble act will herald the advent of a new evil-free *Karan* society. Let me make it clear. Your marriage with *Indumati* will put an immediate stop to all animosity and legal disputes between the families. You have read how the bond of love between Romeo and Juliet had united the warring Capulet and Montague families in Shakespeare's famous play. Likewise, your wedding with *Indumati* will resolve all issues. The only difference will be that in your case, it will be a happy ending."

"No brother *Sadei*, I don't think it will be that easy," *Govind Chandra* broke in. 'You know how firm father could be. Do you believe he will ever go along with this?"

"Well okay, I admit that uncle will not give his consent. Maybe under worst circumstances, he will disown you, depriving you of any claim over his property. That will not be a big issue. The regular turnover of revenue from the zamindari of *Sankarshan* babu is a lot more than that of our *taluk*. Besides, he also profits a lot through the money lending business. He is an exceptionally rich man with as much wealth kept hidden from view as is public. He has given the word that he will get all his assets registered in your name, liquid and otherwise. Brother *Govind* bears in mind that both *taluk*s will merge together in due course and you will be the sole owner of the entire property. That is guaranteed. Brother mine, you are highly educated. A poet with your talent could hardly be found in the whole of Odisha. Haven't you studied human nature? You are the only son of the uncle, the brilliant moon of the *Sri Karan* family. Will he disown you so easily? Let us for the sake of argument presume that he does that. Even then, he cannot deprive you of his property. The Hindu Law of Inheritance does not permit that. And mind you, I am not concerned about the property factor. Because what you are going to gain through this matrimonial match is beyond the reach of millions of men. How many men in Utkal have a poet for a wife? Just give it a thought before deciding anything. I fully agree with the *Shastra*s that prescribe wholehearted devotion and obedience to the father.

> *Pita swarga pita dharma pita hin parama tapah*
> *Pitari pritimapanne priyante sarba devatah*

(Your father is your Heaven, the epitome of Justice; he is the ultimate ascetic pursuit. You can please all the gods if you please your father.)

But that does not mean that in the process of pleasing the father, one should do something which his conscience does not approve of. Is it wise to unthinkingly obey the father who ignores his own conscience, guided by blind convictions asks you to do something that will destroy the peace of your life? That harm the society? That will impede the progress of the nation? Such an injudicious act will, in the long run, cause him harm because whatever effect, either harmful or beneficial, brought in to you by your actions will also influence the life of your father.

It is standard practice in our society while negotiating a matrimonial relationship to inquire about the social and financial status of the families of the prospective groom and bride. While the parents do that, the kinsmen and relatives of both families examine the class and caste aspects. People distantly involved in the process are only interested in the wedding feast. No one ever cares to know about the conduct and the educational qualification of the bride. Let us consider the recent developments in connection with your marriage. Has anyone ever bothered to know if this girl uncle has selected for you is right for you in all aspects? I have heard that the girl cannot even read. After she enters the family as a bride, she won't be able to speak to anyone properly and communicate only with gestures and some inarticulate sounds. Who knows, she might even walk hunched. What's more, you won't find an opportunity to meet her before midnight. The only positive quality in her is that she comes from a *Srikaran* family. But how long that will hold ground? How can an educated and well-read young man be happy with a life partner as innate and useless as a stone? Will not such a mindless act be suicidal? One who submits to such injustice when a favorable alternative is within reach does not deserve any sympathy.

Brother *Govind* listen to me carefully. During the past month, I have been inquiring into the details of the daughter of the zamindar *Sankarshan Mahanty*. She will be the most befitting match for you. A girl as beautiful as her and as educated and talented could be hardly found in all the *Srikaran* families. She can paint and write emotionally evocative poems. She has all the virtues an educated young man expects in a bride. Well, I have to let you know my opinions. Now it is up to you to make your decision. Do not blame me in the future if you are unhappy."

The advice and admonitions made the *kuanr*'s head spin. He found himself caught in a terrible dilemma. A teaching came to his mind – something his teachers cited while he was in the Mission School,

"One may have to desert his parents to live with his wife."

"I can't think clearly. You decide what should be best in the present circumstances," *Kuanr Govind Chandra* said.

"You know a noble mission could be hindered by many obstacles. It will be wise to set to work once we have made our decision," *Sadananda* conciliated.

"Then meet *Rajiv babu* without wasting any time and work out a plan," agreed with the trusting *kuanr*.

"Okay, I will go right away. You go back home. Be careful about *Saita*. He must not smell anything. I know you like him a lot but that fool of a barber might spread the news around. You know that too many confidantes are likely to spoil the secret. So be careful!"

CHAPTER - 18
RAJIVLOCHANA AND KAMALALOCHAN

"How did you like my speech *Rajivlochan babu*?" asked *Kamallochan*. "Wasn't it a brainwasher? Have patience; give it two more speeches and he will be flattened. Do you think I just sit there in the evenings behind a closed door and do nothing? It took me more than a week to prepare that speech. I was so preoccupied with the thought of preparing the speeches that I was unable to pay attention to my studies. But please report the details of my speech to your uncle when you write to him. Tell him that there is no need of doing anything else to accomplish our purpose. The speeches will be enough. Didn't you see how the boys you have put here in this house providing them with free food and shelter got cold feet and kept mum at the appropriate time? Don't you worry. Write to your uncle that he should harbor no apprehension regarding the issue. I will take care of everything." *Rajivlochan* smiled his appreciation.

"But there is something else I want to ask of you," *Kamallochan* resumed. "You know about my financial condition. At your insistence, I devoted most of my time preparing convincing speeches to motivate the *kuanr*. For that, I had to give up the private tuitions I was giving school kids. The payment from those tuitions sustained me. All my expenses including college fees, boarding charges, books, and clothing were met with the money I obtained from it. I also had to send a meager amount to my parents from the tuition fees. We had earlier agreed on the payments for my services. I am not asking for the payment now. But the little money you gave me has been spent. You see, I am totally broke. I'm only requesting you to lend me two hundred rupees to settle my debts. My parents are sending me money in a few days and I can use some of that to pay you back. But now I am badly in need of some money," *Kamallochan* urged.

Rajivlochan replied, "As you can see for yourself *Kamallochan babu*, my hands are tied. I can't even afford to manage household expenses. But don't you worry. Tomorrow, I will send someone to my uncle with a letter. They will then return with the money from *Samsharpur* within a few days. You will be paid as soon as he gets here."

"Write to your uncle in detail about how effective my speech was. And let him know my next one will be even better," said *Kamallochan*.

CHAPTER - 19
GOOD NEWS

The temple of lord *Vinod Vihari*, the tutelary deity of the zamindar family of *Samsharpur* was washed clean and sanctified. The main entrance to the temple or the Lion's Gate, the side entrance and the exit door opening to the adjacent mango grove were kept chained and locked. Pairs of sentries stood guard at different points in the temple premises to prevent entry to unwanted visitors. In the front hall of the main temple sat zamindar *Sankarshan Mahanty*, the priest *Biswanath Satpathy*, *Chhamukarana Srikantha Patnaik* and the astrologer *Bhaskara Kahadiratne*. They were discussing something serious and secret.

"Khadiratne!" the zamindar *sa'anta* asked, "Isn't there an auspicious day this month for solemnizing the marriage?"

Khadiratne leafed through the almanac once again and perused for some time. "There is no auspicious time for marriage throughout this year, let alone this month my lord!" he replied. "We will be able to figure out a date when the new almanac comes out the next year."

The *sa'anta* looked disappointed. The priest *Biswanath Satpathy* was a man of experience; he had good knowledge of the *sashtra*s and the principles prescribed therein. He noticed the disappointment on the zamindar's face and said,

"But the rubrics could be altered in exceptional cases. Our princess has become nubile, she is also motherless. The rules applicable to her case need not be so stringent."

The *sa'anta* turned his eyes to the astrologer.

"Yes, yes, the texts on astrology also say so," *Bhaskara Kahadiratne* echoed enthusiastically. "In fact, I have heard of some instances where such exceptions were permitted by my uncle himself. It could have been endorsed if he were here."

"If it is so, consult the almanac and fix an appropriate and auspicious day for the marriage," the *sa'anta* suggested.

"It would have been better if I had both the birth-charts with me. But no problem, I can manage without one," the astrologer said. He took out a piece of chalk from the waist-fold of his dhoti cast a horoscope of the zamindar's daughter on the floor indicating the position of various planets in it. He also drew her birth chart and put figures inside the houses. The astrologer then studied the horoscope very carefully, touching a few points in it with his finger and deliberating over it for quite a long time. He put down the chalk at last and looked at the zamindar and the priest.

"Right now, our bride to be is under the influence of Jupiter. The lord of wealth now occupies a high position in the house of Cancer. To be precise, the impacts of all other planets are overshadowed by the auspicious influence of Jupiter. The present configuration in her horoscope spells out the most propitious time for her marriage." The astrologer once more began scanning the planetary positions to decide the favorable time and day for the marriage.

Drawing more figures and deliberating for some more time he tried to tally the timing with the position of planets in the horoscope. At last, he raised his face to look the zamindar in the eye and said, "I can find only one day that will be the most auspicious: the fifth day in the fortnight of the moon's bright phase in the month of Aries, that is this Friday. The most favorable time for joining the palms of the bride and the groom in the bond of wedlock will be somewhere before midnight."

"Glory be thine, O' Lord Vinod Vihari! Bless us O'Lord!" the *sa'anta* exclaimed in excess of joy. He lay prostrate on the floor and offered his gratitude. The others joined him in the prostrate position and chanted the name of lord Vinod Vihari. The zamindar *sa'aanta* said, "We have only five days in our hand to make the preparations. I must warn you to keep the plan top secret. No one, I repeat, no one here must get a sniff of it. The palace cashier and the priest will have to leave for Cuttack this very night. No one else, neither a laborer nor a farm-hand of our *taluk* should accompany him. They will carry cash from here and purchase everything required for the institution from Cuttack including the flowers, the *doob* grass, and the *barkoli* leaves. Laborers and luggage carriers will be hired from Cuttack for carrying things to our palace. Be careful about the timing. Everyone and everything must arrive here by the evening of the day of the wedding, that is, this coming Friday. Hand out advances for different varieties of firecrackers, decorative-lighting and an orchestra band. Also, hire a few troupes of dancer-boys for a performance. Try to get the boys' troupe of *Bhingarpur*. They are good. Pay them whatever they charge, don't haggle. Besides these, you should also remember the three most important points in this connection:

'Do not bother about the expenses.'

'Maintain absolute secrecy. No one at Cuttack must know anything about it.'

'Reach here with all the materials required for the wedding by Friday evening.'"

He paused to look at the priest and the cashier to ensure he was heard and resumed," The orchestra band and the lighting procession, however, should start from Cuttack early Friday evening. They should arrive at ten o'clock at night. Guides will be placed at different crossroads to lead them here. The drums, trumpets, and firecrackers in the meantime, should be kept ready, secretly of course, by the time the band arrives. The drummers will start beating the drums as soon as they get the signal from me. All the decorative lights will be lit all at once. The fifty or so tree-shaped firecrackers decorated on either side of the street will be ignited simultaneously. The *mouza Radhikadeipur* at the extreme eastern limits of the *taluk Samsharpur* touches the borders of *mouza GobindaRaypur* of *taluk Dashagram*. Arrange for a few of the large firecrackers to go off in *Radhikadeipur* too. Instruct our people there to set fire to those crackers as soon as they hear the firecrackers from here. The sound should be loud enough to startle the people in the *taluk Dashagram* out of their sleep.

And be careful! Do not exchange a single word with your co-travelers or any strangers on the way back."

He turned to look at the priest and the palace cashier and said, "Listen, both of you, I pin my trust in you and you only. I am repeatedly cautioning you do not let anybody else know of this or else the whole will be ruined."

CHAPTER - 20
PREPARATIONS FOR THE JOURNEY

It was the fourth day of the bright lunar fortnight. The evening had deepened into the night and the moon had advanced well on its way to the west. A horse-driven coach rattled on to the gate of the house at Buxi Bazar. *Rajivlochan babu* hurried out of the main door and welcomed the two young men in the coach effusively, in all smiles. He assisted them in getting out of the coach and led them through the main gate. A shabbily dressed man who looked like a servant was sitting next to the driver of the coach. After the two passengers went inside, he too slowly got down and entered through the gate. After the coach drove away *Rajivlochan* locked the front door of the ground floor unit and led the two guests up the stairs to the second floor. Three young men who had been waiting there came forward smiling broadly to greet them. They welcomed the guests wishing them a good evening in a very polite manner, shook their hands and sat them in a couple of chairs by a large table. The shabby-looking man who had accompanied the two young men sat in the kitchen with the cooks and the servants. The young men exchanged pleasantries with one another and engaged in polite small talk. Not long after, someone asked *Kamallochan babu* to sing a song. Without waiting for further persuasion

Kamallochan sat down by the harmonium. He played a tune on its reeds and began singing:

> "Go to *Shyma* o' *sakhi,* and make haste,
> Clinging to the hope to be with him, here I wait;
>
> He must come here this *dasi* to meet,
> He must take mercy on me, pray to him I hold his feet;
>
> It is for him to my family I have brought disgrace,
> Longing for *Shyama* has made me so restless;
>
> He is the storehouse of the jewel of love
> My life without him is meaningless,
> Let him know how I suffer, and beg him to come
> Or else I will end my life."

Kamallochan himself was the lyricist and composer. He was well skilled in all arts. He could sing nicely to the tune of musical instruments. He had a melodious voice. He could play several musical instruments. Very few could match his abilities on the tabla. He had also had some practice in dancing. The world, however, was not kind about this. Some such jealous characters whispered behind his back that *Kamallochan* had been a performer in a mere dancer-boy troupe.

The singing and merrymaking went on until it was time for dinner. The dinner, which included several dishes both native and foreign, was prepared by a couple of professional cooks hired for the purpose. There were also fruits and dessert to go with dinner. Before the dinner was laid out *Kamallochan* cleared his throat as if to say something. All eyes turned towards him. "Brothers," he began, "Since we all belong to the *srikaran* caste we can eat from one plate. But our eating habits are very clumsy and involve activities that could be easily dispensed with. Washing the hands and face, rinsing them dry with a napkin, sitting down on a mat spread out on the floor, getting the food served on plantain leaves, soiling our hand with food while we eat— all these form parts of the ritual of eating. But people in civilized countries follow decent and clean table manners while eating. They don't grub their hands but eat neatly using spoons, knives, and forks. Should we give it a try tonight?"

The young men laughed aloud, clapped and gave their consent. *Rajivlochan babu* rang a bell, and as if they were coached beforehand, two servants hurried to spread out a nice tablecloth on the large table. They neatly arranged the spoons, knives, and forks on folded napkins at the appropriate places for six dinners. Once again *Rajivlochan* rang the small bell and the servants came up carrying the dishes and arranged them on the table. All of the servants he had hired seemed to be professionals in the matter. The six young men talked and laughed while enjoying the delicious dishes that emitted an inviting aroma. While the young men were busy eating and no one noticed *Sadananda* and *Rajivlochan's* eyes speaking in signals. Halfway through the dinner *Rajivlochan* spoke looking at his friends, "Brothers let us finalize tomorrow's program. We are not as disciplined as the people of civilized countries. We are not accustomed to making proper plans prior to a journey and hence we fuss over everything just at the nick of the moment. Lack of orderliness always messes up everything. Let us plan out everything neatly for tomorrow's journey to *Samsharpur*. I have arranged for half a dozen palanquin bearers to be waiting with six palanquins in the courtyard below. Eight others, who will be carrying the luggage in baskets hanging from the split bamboo staves levered on their shoulders, also will be waiting there. They will carry our luggage and personal effects. We will start before the break of dawn, at the auspicious hour when the temple bells will begin ringing. All the palanquins will have been marked and you all must find your own and get in without creating any confusion. We will be reaching the grove at Gopalpur sometime after sunrise."

Kamallochan babu continued, "All arrangements are made there. The cooks and provisions will all be ready by the time we arrive. The place is neat and clean. You won't find even a dry leaf under the trees. A river flows by the grove which enhances the picturesque beauty of the landscape. The water in the river is crystal clear. It will be fun swimming in the river. Arrangements also have been made for a game of dice which you can enjoy after lunch and a short rest. I am carrying the harmonium box with me. I will entertain you while you all play."

Govindchandra looked enquiringly at *Sadananda*. Perhaps he was a little confused at all the detailed planning and preparations. *Rajivlochan,* reading the mind of the *kuanr* said quickly, "*Kuanr babu,* our uncle, the zamindar *sa'anta* had repeatedly cautioned that one of us, whoever is clever as well as trustworthy, will have to remain here. The errand boys from the village will be coming here time and again carrying orders from him. Only brother *Sadananda* can handle such matters. I have requested him to stay back and take care of everything. A palanquin along with the palanquin bearers will be kept waiting. Brother *Sadananda* will start from here as soon as he receives my message. What do you say brother *Sadananda*?' He looked at *Sadananda* as if seeking an answer."

"Of course!" *Sadananda* assured. "How can I disobey

your uncle's instructions? He is a respected senior in our community. Won't he take it amiss? He may not speak of it, but he will think that the young men of today who have learned English do not know proper manners. I would never disobey his orders."

CHAPTER - 21
THE WEDDING CEREMONY

The people in *Binodpur mouza* in the *taluk Samsharpur,* where the zamindar's palace was situated were curious. They had guessed that something important was about to happen in the palace. Many close associates and the ministerial staff of the zamindar *sa'aanta* were engaged in a flurry of activities. They never talked about anything out loud but communicated only with gestures and whispers.

Errand boys were hurrying to and back from the Cuttack road carrying secret letters at quick intervals. Early that morning, around a hundred guards were posted on different streets of the village. There were strict orders from the zamindar that no one, not even a child could leave the village. There was, however, not much restriction on people coming into the village. Pairs of sentries stood guard at the foreyard and at the back entrance of the palace. No woman was permitted to enter or leave the palace.

The zamindar was pacing about the palace looking restless. He had not taken his bath at his usual time nor had performed the daily morning worship. Time and again he was coming out of the palace gate and kept looking at the Cuttack Road. Around midday, a couple of guards all drenched in sweat were seen striding towards the palace. Reaching the palace gate, they handed a letter to the *sa'anta.*

The zamindar glanced at the contents of the letter and a smile lit up his face. The ministerial staff and his trusted followers noticed his reaction and came hurrying. "The palanquins have arrived at the right spot," the zamindar said smiling his relief. Only then did he resume his schedule and went away to take his bath.

It was after dusk. The sound of the conches signaled auspicious ululations throughout the palace. The evening lamps were lit in most of the houses in the *mouza Binodpur.* The rest of the houses were about to light their evening lamps. The call of the palanquin bearers was heard at a distance from the direction of the Cuttack Road. The activities in the palace had gathered a sudden momentum. The blowing of conches and the auspicious ululations filled the air once more.

The zamindar *sa'anta* along with the head priest *Biswunalh Salpathy* and some Brahmin priests entrusted with the task of receiving the bridegroom walked out of the main entrance.

There were two groups of torchbearers carrying flaming torches. While one group moved ahead of the zamindar's entourage the other brought up the rear. The zamindar wore a silk white dhoti with triangle-shaped designs of deep, bright colors along its border. A mantle, folded neatly to look like a band went up across his chest, passed over his left shoulder to reach his right side and was wound around his waist. On the ring finger of his right hand, he wore a length of *kush* grass knotted to form a ring.

As soon as the gong of the evening worship sounded in the temple of Lord *Vinod Vihari,* the palanquin bearers put down the six palanquins in a row in front of the main entrance to the palace. The receiving priests followed by the zamindar *Sankarshan Mahanty* walked up to *kuanr*

Govind Chandra's palanquin, chanting slokas from the *Vedas* in one voice. *Rajivlochan* quickly climbed down from one of the palanquins and helped the other four to get down from their respective ones. They joined the priests around the palanquin of the *kuanr.*

The palanquin of the *kuanr* was about six cubits long with colorful patterns drawn along its panels. The front was made of silver designed in the shape of a crocodile's mouth. The interior was lined with gold- brocaded velvets. A comfortable velvet-cushioned bed was laid out inside the palanquin. An awning of velvet for the palanquin, rolled neatly, was kept on its roof. *Rajivlochan* slid opened the door-panels of the palanquin. Two barbers layout a silver tub, a silver sitting-board and a silver water-pot in front of it. They lay a new white napkin, folded on the top of the water pot and moved back.

Rajivlochan opened the door at the back of the palanquin a little and whispered in *GovindCahandra's* ear, "You should push away uncle's hands respectfully when he bends down to wash your feet. It is just a ritual, understand?"

The groom stepped down ceremoniously. The priests began the ritual of receiving the groom at the entrance of the bride's home. The head priest chanted slokas from the Vedas.

"*Aagachha mama bakyena bhujyatam subhamuttamam*

Kadami kanyaka danam subhena gamyata kulam."

(At my request you have come let everything be auspicious happen to you Receive the gift of my daughter and return all well and happy.)

The bride's father poured the turmeric water contained in the silver water pot on the groom's feet. After putting marks of vermilion and sandalwood paste on his forehead the bride's father slid a garland and a gold chain over the groom's head. Then he put a ring studded with a diamond on his finger. The diamond in the ring coruscated in the light of the torch.

The priests chanted mantras in a chorus:
"Biraja dohasi biraja dohamasiha
Mama padyani biraja doha"

(O Water appear now acquiring a holy glow
I now chant mantras to sanctify you
May you in your hallowed form cleanse my feet;)

They walked ahead followed by the groom and the bride's father who held the right thumb of his would-be son-in-law. The groom's friends from Cuttack walked behind them in a cheery mood.

The groom was this way ceremoniously ushered into a large hall and was made to sit on a gaudily decorated seat. From the huge beam across the ceiling hung huge candelabrums from which multiple holders for the candles stemmed out in ornate designs. Similarly designed sconces were clamped to the walls on all sides of the big hall. The light from the candelabra glinted off the gold-spun cushion covers strewing luminous specks all around the hall. The groom sat still as a statue, holding his head down.

The renowned troupes of dancer-boys from Cuttack and Puri had arrived and were busy in doing their make-up. The entertainment would begin shortly. "Just play romantic songs tonight," *Rajivlochan* whispered in the ears of the troupe managers. Around ten bottles containing perfumes and rose water were placed in front of the bridegroom's seat. At short intervals, *Rajivlochan* sprinkled rose water over the people assembled in the hall. Cotton wool buds wrapped around small sticks were dipped into the perfume and touched to their clothes. So much of rose water was sprinkled on the gathering that the articles of clothing of many were soaking wet. Betel leaves containing spices were folded into neat cones were placed on a couple of big silver platters as palette cleansers for the guests.

Rajivlochan, with a folded scarf, hung over his shoulder, approached the groom and spoke respectfully in a low voice, "Will you kindly accompany me to the adjoining room?" Although *Rajivlochan* was an old acquaintance and a friend, such formalities were to be observed on occasions like this. Holding the groom's right hand *Rajivlochan* led him to another large room. This room too was brilliantly lit. A number of silver and gold gilt chairs were placed along its walls. An ornate round table stood in the middle of the room. A coarse sheet was spread over the entire floor. A fluffy carpet imported from Teheran was laid over the sheet. A set of groom's clothing that contained a turban with ornamental *Banarasi* designs stitched on it, a full-sleeved flashy long coat reaching to the knees and similarly fashioned trousers were placed on the table. *Rajivlochan* requested the *kuanr* to wear them. *Govind Chandra* was feeling shy and discomfited, but *Rajivlochan* urged him very humbly. "It's a necessity of all the wedding rituals," he said trying to convince the groom. At last, with a lot of hesitation, the *kuanr* changed into his wedding apparel. He walked back to the court hall, looking more handsome and elegant. Everyone was filled with joy at the grandeur and resplendence.

The rituals at the altar of marriage had begun. After offering worship to the forefathers some priests stood around the altar. Amidst the chanting of the mantras, they began the ritual of winding up of the sacred thread which was to be used as the wedlock-bond. The palms of the bride and the groom were joined together, and the sacred bond was rolled around them as the priest chanted:

"*Jatha Indrasya Indrani*
Jatha Nalasya Damayanti
> *Jatha Saudasasya Madayanti*
> *Jatha Ravanasya Mandodari*
> *Jatha Dhritarashtrasya Gandhari* "

(As the perfect pair of Indra and Indrani, of Nala and Damayanti, Saudasa and Madayanti, Ravan and Mandodari, Dhritarashtra and Gandhari)

A wave of electric current ran through the bride and the bridegroom as both of their hands were held together in the sacred wedlock-bond in the same way a pair of cloud layers facing each other streaks of lightning flashed out simultaneously and merged in each other. Both felt that not only their bodies but their souls were now united forever.

Their hands were still held together as the auspicious moment to unwind the thread was still a few minutes away when the earsplitting sound of hundreds of firecrackers bursting at the mango grove at the end of the village tore the air around. Almost instantly the hands and sticks struck at the drums in a rhythmic beat and the lights designed in attractive shapes were kindled. The firecrackers boomed in village *Gobindraypur* at the same time. The perfect synchronization of the firecrackers bursting in both villages, the kindling of the lights and the beating of the drums created a grandiosity that was phenomenal. People in the villages around who did not have the slightest inkling of the reality were scared out of their wits at the unusual sound and the iridescence. The booming of the firecrackers sent a tremor through the village. Dust and loose earth came hurtling down from the thatched ceilings. All the villagers, men, women, and children were startled out of their sleep and hurried outdoors. Young brides and maidens, driven by curiosity and fear rushed outside ignoring all propriety of conduct to join the confused crowd. Luckily it was dark outside or else their improper manners might have brought disrepute to them. Fear prevented the villagers from thinking logically and they just ran helter-skelter, adding to the commotion.

The wedlock-bond was unwound signaling the sound of conches blowing and ululations. The scared village mob immediately interpreted the sound like something familiar, belonging to a religious ritual to stop some disaster. Earthquake!! The truth struck everyone like a lightning flash. It must be an earthquake and that was why they kept hearing the sound of conches and ululations! They also joined the sound loudly praying and calling out *Haribol*. Within half an hour, the sound traveled a full circle enfolding all the villages around. The female-folk in the zamindar's palace at *Chandanpur*, the attending maids and the *sa'antani* herself came out, half-dazed, and began to blow conches and ululated.

No one knew for sure what happened. But everyone had guessed that an earthquake had hit the area. Small children, frightened enough to cry, gripped the saris of their mothers and kept gaping at their faces. The zamindar *sa'anta* in the palace at *Chandanpur* too, thoroughly alarmed, strode to the temple of Lord *Govinda jiu* and ordered the priests and the other servitors at the temple to blow the pipe and conches and sound the gong. He too had guessed that it was an earthquake.

Meanwhile, in the palace of the zamindar of

Samsharpur, the wedding ceremony was over. The young men of Cuttack who had accompanied the groom had freshened up after their journey and were sitting in a large, extravagantly decorated hallway which led to the interior of the palace. The young men sat around a big circular table sipping their morning tea. They were engaged in small talk, directing their light and playful remarks mostly at the groom, *Govind Chandra.* The rituals of the marriage were completed but the zamindar *sa'anta* was not at rest. He was constantly haunted by undefined misgivings. The trust of the bridegroom would have to be won over and he would have to keep him in control, he decided. He walked into the hallway and stood by the table. The young men stood up respectfully. "Sit down my boys," the zamindar said. "As you can see, I have become old. My days are numbered. I have pinned all my hopes on my son *Govind Chandra.* He will carry forward my family. He will be the sole owner of all my property. I have made up my mind to withdraw from worldly affairs. *Govind* will take over as soon as he completes his studies at Cuttack." The zamindar *sa'anta* sighed, his voice moist with emotion and walked slowly out.

CHAPTER - 22

It was too early in the morning. The sun-god had yet to make his appearance in the east. People of the villages around half-walked, half-ran to the *Chandanpur* palace. They knew that the palace housed a good number of men of practical wisdom. Whenever the people in the nearby villages had any doubts on any subject they approached the knowledgeable men in the palace of the zamindar *Baishnaba Charana Patnaik* to get it cleared. They must know what caused this incident hitherto unseen and unheard of. And so, the villagers hurried; some of them had washed and brushed their teeth while others came straight from their beds, not even bothering to change their clothes. The tremor lasted for nearly an hour and not just the earth, but the sky had appeared to be shaking. There was no storm or rain but the deafening sound of thunderclaps tore through the air.

Zamindar *Baishnaba Charana Patnaik* sat in the temple premises surrounded by many elderly and senior *karanas*, Brahmins and pundits of the village, most of who had arrived there without waiting to be summoned. There were also a group of servants and hirelings waiting to take orders from their master. "Tell us *Bidyanidhi*," the zamindar said turning to the pundit," What kind of earthquake was this? Why would the sky shake during an earthquake?"

Pundit *Kashinath Bidyanidhi* closed his eyes and pondered the question for a bit. He finally opened them and replied, "Your Highness, it is mentioned in the *Utpatasagara Sashtra* what sort of impact such unusual incidents might cause. The sky and the earth-shaking simultaneously is a bad omen. It spells disaster for the country. Your Highness is aware of what a great pundit my old uncle *Gadei Tihadi* was. He would have predicted the same thing."

"I have heard it as well," endorsed *Bhimsen Tihadi.*

The astrologer Khadiratna joined them, "Yes Your Highness, the pundits have interpreted it correctly. I got out of bed as soon as I felt the first shock of the tremor and opened the almanac. I found it written there that on the fifth day of the bright lunar-fortnight, a Friday, the zodiac sign of Taurus would come under the influence of the *Mrigashira* star for a brief period, about less than an hour. It would have an evil influence on the atmosphere. Shock waves generating from the north-west quarter of the earth would travel through the air in the north-east direction. The impact will last for an hour or so. This incident forebodes bad times for the people and the country."

Over at the *taluka* of *Samsharpur,* the zamindar had carefully organized things to suit his purpose. He had paid money to some of the watchmen at the common border of the two talukas, *Dashagram* and *Samsharpur,* and instructed them to spread out the news of the marriage as soon as the ceremony is over. The zamindar had opened his treasury and did not spare any expenses as the occasion was an exceptionally special one. "Money can perform miracles," they say. So the watchmen acted as per the instruction of zamindar *Shankarshan Mahanty* and let the news travel around.

As the zamindar of *Dashagram* sat in the temple premises with the astrologers and other elderly men of his village discussing the possible cause and effect of the strange earthquake, the watchman of *mouza Gopala* of the *taluka Somarayapur* came running to the temple gate. He stood there, his staff over his shoulder, breathing hard. "Your Majesty!" he said with much effort. "Last night the *kuanr sa'aanta* and the daughter of the zamindar of *Samsharpur* were married!"

At first, the zamindar and others did not comprehend. The watchman repeated what he had said. He hadn't finished repeating as another guard came after him and announced the same thing. It took a little time to sink in with the zamindar. But when it did, it created the impact of another earthquake, much, much more powerful. A hundred thunderbolts striking the place at one time would not have been as shocking as the news. Such was the enormity of disbelief that it left everyone there numb and paralyzed. They sat still like wooden statues looking blankly at one another's face.

In the meantime, the news, like torrents of water rushing downhill after the first rain in the month of *Asadha*, had flooded into every house in every village of *taluka Dashagram*. The zamindar *sa'anta* sat very still, his vacant eyes fixed on the distant skyline. One could not be sure if he was within his senses or not. The sun had risen quite high up in the sky, but no one rose. How could they when their master and lord sat there like a statue? The errand-runners and the watchmen also stood still, speechless, holding their staves over their shoulders. At last *Bidei Mahanty*, an old *Karana* who was close to the zamindar raised him holding his arm and took him inside the palace.

Inside, he went to take a shower and then went to the

prayer room. He stood in front of lord *Gobinda jiu* with folded hands.

"O my son *GobindaChandra*!" he said addressing the deity. "Is this your doing? Of course, you have done it? Who else? Don't I know that even a leaf of grass won't flutter unless you will so? I am a puny, ignorant creature. I do not have the ability to decipher your intricate designs. But you know that I have no one to lean on other than you. Generation after generation my family had sought shelter at your kind feet. How could you reduce my reputation to dust so abruptly in this manner? Well then! Let it be so if you want it that way!" The zamindar muttered accusingly in a voice soaked in unshed tears.

It was peculiar that the *sa'anta* addressed the deity as his son. It so happened that the zamindar couple had remained childless for many years. In the end, they decided to adopt their tutelary deity as their son by performing a *Yajna* called the *putresthi yajna*. So, in the religious sense, they adopted the deity as their son and the zamindar had written down his land and other properties in the name of the deity. Except for reserving the right of spending a certain amount on the food offering made to the deity that befits a servitor, the zamindar never spent even a paisa from the property designated in the Lord's name. There were several *mouza*s in the name of the zamindar's wife, the *sa'antani*. The zamindar couple met the occasional and sundry expenses with the revenue-income from these *mouza*s.

He had truly believed and lived that relationship between him and his diety. Someone overhearing the *sa'anta* while he recounted his problems and pains aloud standing before the deity could very well mistake it for a father speaking to his son.

The *sa'antani* was standing at the entrance to the inner

section of the palace listening to the domestic maids discussing the earthquake when someone brought in the news of the *kuanr*'s marriage. As soon as she heard the news, an indistinct moan escaped her and she fell on the floor, unconscious. The maids rushed in, cradled her up in their arms and carried the *sa'antani* to her bedroom. They laid her carefully on her bed, sprinkled water on her face and fanned her. After a while, the *sa'antani* opened her eyes, but the shock was so strong that no words came out of her mouth. The news had devastated her.

For the past year, the *sa'antani*'s mind was filled with the thoughts of her only son's marriage. She would choose a girl of divine beauty for her son and the marriage ceremony would be performed with great pomp and splendor as befits a prince. She would daydream of the making of jewelry, buying clothes, and the different kinds of invitations to be sent out to different relatives and kinsmen depending upon the degree of closeness and respectability. Fate perhaps was smiling at the naivety of this poor mother as she flattered herself with such imaginations. A human being, a puny, ignorant creature, living within the limits of the present time can never see beyond it. Blind to what future stores for him, he is constantly engaged in the futile act of building a domain of dreams. What the Ultimate Being who is infinite and immortal ordains for him is beyond his limited powers of perception and hence often causes pain and suffering. But the Lord always works out plans for us that prove beneficial in the long run. Doesn't a boy that whiles away valuable time in playing allege his father of cruelty when the latter punishes him and forces him to engage himself in his studies? Whatever the father does is for a better future for the son, but the boy's small mind cannot fathom the father's intention. We, ordinary humans, disabled by our ignorance and limitedness, fail to fathom the mysterious intentions of the Ultimate Being who always designs things for the wellbeing of His most loved creation, and moan and wail and blame Him. Prompted by our ignorance and insufficient knowledge we often misconstrue the designs of our merciful Supreme Father and mourn our loss.

The news of the *kuanr's* wedding was a bolt from the blue. It annihilated all happy hopes and dreams the zamindar couple had nurtured relating to their only son's marriage. No one saw the *sa'antani* strolling in the courtyard of the palace or engaged in a lighthearted conversation with anyone after the devastating news was received. A graveyard silence reigned in the palace. The court hall of the zamindar *sa'anta* which often throbbed with lively chatter wore a deserted look. People seldom came to visit the hall now. A subject happening to pass by the palace by chance would now bow a grim head and move away quietly. The *Samantas* of the *Srikaran* society sat in small groups at different places in the village holding their heads down in abject humiliation. "What a terrible thing the boy did!!" they said to one another in utter disappointment. "He has ruined the pride and honor of the *Srikaran* society!"

CHAPTER - 23

In his last days, the poet Madhusudan had written a line that became very popular in later times.

"The male frog says to his mate
Every instant this world changes-"

A human being is the tiniest part of this world where change is a constant and frequent occurrence. His life is conditioned by cosmic law. Impermanence is the strongest characteristic of all events that occur in human life. The intense hostility between the heads of the two *Karan* zamindars and the overpowering enthusiasm with which both kept filing lawsuits against each other were significantly mellowed just in the manner a leaping flame is doused when water is poured on it. The disputes which had all been pending in court were getting dismissed one after another owing to the absence of the disputants or their representatives on the scheduled dates of hearings. A few months before the wedding, the two *Karan sa'anta*s growled at each other like two angry dogs when they chanced upon each other. But now they were quietly avoiding each other and changed course. Anyone intently observing the look on the face of each could easily decipher the state of their minds. While one of them walked slowly his head lowered under a load of sorrow and humiliation the other moved to hide his triumphant joy behind a serious veneer.

CHAPTER - 24

Time never waits for anyone. Days had incessantly flowed on through the grim somberness of *taluka Dashagram* and the rejoicing and celebration in the *taluka* of *Samsharpur*. Four months had passed since the marriage of *kuanr Govind Chandra*. In the last four months, the zamindar *Samanta Baishnaba Charan Patnaik Bidyadhar Mahapatra* had completely withdrawn himself from public life. He spent most of the time in the temple of lord *Gobinda jiu*. The cooks and the errand boys, as well as some of the zamindar's close associates often heard him talking to the deity. Barely anyone ventured to approach him. Rarely would someone very close to him gather enough courage to speak to the zamindar sa'anta if at all he seemed to be in the right mood.

The *sa'antani* most of the time, lay in bed nursing her grief. She did not speak to anyone. The attendant maids helped her in the morning routine. She had in the meantime forgotten and forgiven the wrongdoing of her son. Day and night, she was obsessed with the desire to see her son. "Send for my *Govind* just once. I want to see him," she would say. But her husband never mentioned their son after that fateful day. The indifference of the zamindar had filled the *sa'antani* with terrible apprehensions. But she was an ideal wife and like any ideal and chaste wife, she revered and obeyed her husband. Despite a compelling urge to see her son the *sa'antani* did not have the courage to send for him fearing it would hurt her husband's sentiments. Most women, it is seen, are influenced more strongly by their love for their children than the dutifulness for their husbands. But the *sa'antani* was different. She did not go against her husband's will, but the repressed desire took a toll on her health. Her life was utterly distracted. Disturbed sleep, an irregular morning routine, and insufficiency of food had made her sick. Her fever got worse by each passing day. That morning the *Raja Vaidya* studied her pulse and expressed his concern. "The symptoms clearly show that she might go into a coma at any time," he said. Men of wisdom say that the desire of a person lying dormant in his subconscious surfaces at the time of death. The *sa'antani* was in a state of delirium and kept on chanting, "Where is my son? Where is *Govind*?" The almanac readers, sat in the outer hall discussing the problem, "The sa'anta must be told about this and allow us to fetch *kuanra babu* from Cuttack. That is our last hope. Or else the *sa'antani* will not live."

CHAPTER - 25
SADANANDA'S RETROSPECTION

In Cuttack, *Sadananda* was congratulating himself on his manipulative skill. "Bah!" he thought happily. How tactfully had he handled the situation! He had not attended the marriage on purpose. Nobody in the *taluka Dashagram* could accuse him of participating in the event. *Govinda* perhaps would have taken amiss to his absence. But he had successfully managed to convince him. He had simply said to *Rajivlochan* that he found out that some people from the *Chandanpur* palace were coming to Cuttack to meet them. If they did not find anyone here, they might smell a conspiracy. They might rush to *Samsharpur* and spoil the whole game. They could easily influence *Govinda* to change his mind. No, someone responsible had to stay back and explain things convincingly. If they inquired, he would say that *Govind* had gone to Puri and detain them here for some time, or he might just travel to Puri along with them. That will give them ample time to execute their plan. Neither *Rajivlochan* nor *Govind* could ever figure out what his real intentions were. None of them can blame or misunderstand him. *Govind* had himself had requested him to stay back to handle things in case of an emergency. He had successfully kept himself in the clear. If his uncle and aunt asked him why he did not stop *Govind* he could always convince them by saying that he had no inkling of his planning. He would convince them that wouldn't he have informed them had he the slightest knowledge of it?

As he tried to reconstruct the incidents the way he wanted them to be reported, a disturbing thought crossed his mind. *Govind* was sure to misunderstand him once he realized that he had lied to his parents about his involvement in the wedding. He must see to it that *Govind* did not get reconciled with his parents in the near future. He should be stopped from going to his father's palace at *Chandanpur*. He was a stubborn boy and would not change his mind easily. But the rift that had occurred between the father and son must be widened by craft. He would have to make sure that his uncle would not ask *Govind* to come to the palace nor would *Govind* go there unasked.

CHAPTER - 26
BROTHERS

"What are you thinking about so seriously sitting on the rooftop all alone?" *Govinda* asked approaching *Sadananda* who looked visibly perturbed.

Nothing, I was a little busy in revising the topics taught in class yesterday. I could not come to you to greet you because of that. Tell me. What's the matter?"

"No, no – there is no such thing as you presume. I am just whiling away time—" replied the cunning Sadanand in a voice that was purposely made to sound disturbed to increase *Govind's* curiosity.

"Forget it. Let's talk about something else."

"No, *Sadei bhai!*" *Govind* said obstinately. "You have to tell me the truth."

"Listen to me carefully my dear *Govind*," said *Sadananda* conciliatorily. "He is your father after all. A father is the image of God. A sensitive and intelligent boy like you should not take it to heart if the father says something unwarranted in a spurt of anger."

"'Stop talking in riddles, please brother!" *Govind* snapped. "Why don't you come straight to the point?"

"Look, how angry you're getting! That was why I did not want to tell you anything. But now since you are forcing me, I have to tell you everything," *Sadananda* took a pause preparing the ground for his lie.

"You know *Makara Mahanty* of our village. I ran into him yesterday afternoon in the *Shahabzada* bazaar. He told me that your father is terribly upset at what you have done. He is so terribly angry with you that he had declared publicly that he would never look you in the face again. '*Govind* has brought disgrace upon my family-name by marrying the daughter of a lowly *Golam Mahanty,* a hybrid *Karan.* He is not my son.' But you must not mind that," *Sadananda* said in a solicitous manner.

"He is an elderly, respectable person and your father. His anger will not last much longer. In a short time, he will get over it and take you in his arms. Now that he is a little disturbed, he is not sending you money for your regular expenses, nor is showing any concern about how you're managing here without money. Did that bring your life to a stop or cause any serious trouble? You have no worries at all. And listen to me; forget about how your father reacted. It does not behoove you to take the words of our superiors seriously."

Govind sat glumly for a few minutes. "*Sadei Bhai* you know that I do not go back on my promises. I will never step in the palace unless and until my father himself comes here and asks me!!" He said with finality.

CHAPTER - 27
LETTER FROM THE PALACE OF *SAMSHARPUR*

Night had fallen. In most of the houses, the evening lamps were lit. *Sadananda babu* and *kuanr Govind Chandra* had returned from their evening stroll at the river bank were preparing to sit down to study. They heard *Rajivlochan* calling them from outside, "Hey *Govinda Chandra babu and Sadananda babu!*" Without waiting for them to come out *Rajivlochan* strode into the house. "We just parted ways with you," said the *kuanr* in surprise. "What happened? What made you come back so urgently?"

"Look at this," said *Rajivlochan* handing him a letter.

"Sadei bhai, would you please read the letter," the *kuanr said* passing the envelope to *Sadananda.*

The latter turned the letter over his palm, looking at both sides of the closed envelope, tore the sealed end open and began reading aloud,

"I seek shelter at the holy feet of the family's tutelary deity Sri Sri Sri *Vinoda Vihari.* I write this on the sixth year of the rule of *Raja Sri Sri Dibyasingh Deb*, after days ten since the sign of cancer had entered the zodiac, the second day of the bright lunar fortnight, Wednesday, about nine in the morning, from the palace of the zamindar of *taluka Samsharpur*, at the orders of His Majesty the zamindar Samanta:

You are to know that last year the paddy crop was blighted by a severe drought in the villages around here. People belonging to the poor and lowly class, failing to fight acute starvation, now have resorted to criminal acts like thieving. Theft takes place almost every night in the villages adjacent to the palace. Last night a theft was reported to have occurred in the village *Similipur*, located just a little distance away from the palace. *Ghana Mahanty, Gobinda Sha* and *Shyama Rana* had broken into three houses of the village and got away with all their valuables. These incidents should have to be reported to the District Magistrate, and the Superintendent of Police. Appeals should be made to them to adopt appropriate security measures like posting police constables on night patrol in this area. The report, however, must be written in English for enabling the Sahibs to go through it without the assistance of an interpreter. As you are aware no one in the villages here has any knowledge of English. Hence His Majesty the zamindar *sa'anta* wants you to come urgently to the village in order to write this report. Take this wish of the zamindar *sa'anta* as his order.

Two palanquins are being sent to Cuttack along with the bearers. You will come to the village in one of them and let the other one along with the four bearers stay back in Cuttack. From what you have mentioned in your earlier letter, only four days of this term of college to close vacation. As soon as the college closes, the *kuanr babu*, our zamindar *sa'anta*'s son-in-law must come to the palace in that palanquin. *Sri* zamindar *samanta* is anxiously waiting to see him. Everyone else in the palace is eagerly waiting for His Majesty *kuanr babu*. What more is there to write? I may be permitted to stop here.

Yours sincerely,
Banchhanidhi Mahanty

The almanac-reader of the palace of the zamindar *Samsharpur.*

They had been listening quietly as the letter was being readout. *Rajivlochan* broke the silence. "I'm assuming that this letter is just a pretext *Govinda babu.* Actually, uncle *sa'anta* wants to discuss something private with you."

"I too feel that you must go to the palace to see what the matter is.," *Sadananda* endorsed *Rajivalochan* immediately.

"Well, okay I will go if you insist," the *kuanr* said resignedly breathing out a deep sigh.

Almost instantly *Rajivalochan* rose to his feet. "I must leave then. I will buy some groceries from the market and set out as early as possible," he said, winking secretly at *Sadananda.* "Wait, *Rajiv Bhai,*" *Sadananda* called. "I will walk you to the gate." IIe followed *Rajivlochan* out of the house and cast a furtive look behind to ascertain no one was within the earshot. "*Rajiv bhai,* please don't forget about me," he said lowering his voice.

"Of course, I will send you the money as soon as I obtain the permission of uncle *sa'anta.* But remember uncle will feel hurt if *Govind* does not come to the palace. If he doesn't, I may not be able to convince him."

CHAPTER - 28

It was Friday evening. The two brothers, *Sadananda babu* and *Govind babu* were walking back from the riverbank. *Sadananda* suddenly caught sight of someone familiar walking towards the house urgently followed by two palanquins carried on by bearers. Even in the dimming light of the dusk, *Sadananda* recognized *Paika Raghu Baghasingh* to accompany the palanquin bearers. He was *Durga Dasa Mahanty*, the *muqaddam* of mouza *Gopalpur*. *Sadananda* became alert immediately. *Kuanr Govind babu* did not see them as he was past the line of sight. *Sadananda* increased his pace and caught up with him. *kuanr Govind Chandra*. "Come on, let's go inside. It is getting late," he said urgently. He ushered *Govind* in and bolted the front door. As *Sadananda* was changing his clothes, he heard someone calling out from the street.

"Saita, Hey Saita, Hey barber boy—"

Not waiting for *Saita* to open the door *Sadananda* came out of his room and opened the front door. "Ohh! *Mahanty!* So it's you!" *Sadananda* said feigning surprise. "What brings you here?"

Durga Dasa Mahanty broke into tears. "Please let me see *kuanr babu*," he said amidst sobs. "It is extremely urgent. Her Majesty the *Sa'antani* is seriously ill. The end may come at any moment. She yearns to see you and the *kuanr.* Please make haste! Ask the *kuanr babu* to leave for the village as early as possible," he begged.

"Well, well— you wait here, I will get *Govind*," said *Sadananda* and went inside closing the door behind him. He turned around to see Govind standing there.

"I have heard everything!" said a perturbed *Govind* as soon as *Sadananda* came inside. "Shall we head out for the village now?"

"My dear brother, don't tell me you really believe what the man said. The fraud is lying through his teeth. Think about it. Wouldn't uncle have sent some errand runner with the message had aunt been so critically ill? Besides, I often come across people from the village in the market. I always ask them if there is any important news about the palace and they always say that everything is well there. When people we know closely haven't said anything, how can we believe a man that is almost a stranger? He has come with two palanquins and palanquin–bearers. And the way he is sobbing! That itself is proof enough that he is feigning. This is a typical characteristic of cheats and liars. He says that he is the *muqaddam*. But I don't know him. Do you?"

"I do not know most of the *Karanas* in the village," said *Govind* a little uncertainly.

"'Exactly!" *Sadananda* said trying to dissuade *Govind* from taking a decision to go to his palace at *Chandanpur*. "Had he been an employee of the zamindar *sa'anta* wouldn't we have recognized him? He is definitely a fraud who came here with some malicious motive."

"No *Sadei bhai*. I am feeling very disturbed. I think we should visit the palace once, just to be sure!" the distressed Govind replied.

"Well, Fine…we must go there if the aunt is ill. I insist that we should go there. Don't you know how dearly aunt loves me! So, don't ever think that I am not concerned. But no one from *Jhankad* I have met recently has ever mentioned any such incident. I am not sure if I can trust this man. But even then, we must visit the palace at least once to be sure that everything is fine there." *Sadananda* paused here to think.

"Yes, I have an idea that will best suit our purpose," he said arriving at a solution. "You proceed directly for *Samsharpur* now. I will leave for our village early tomorrow morning. I will send an errand-runner immediately over to you with the information if anyone in the palace, let alone your mother, is ill. At *Samsharpur,* plan to keep a boat docked and ready to sail at the shortest notice. Set sail as soon as you get the news. At this time of the year, there might be strong currents in the river close to the banks on both sides. But it is relatively calm in between. You will be able to reach at the bathing *ghat* of our village by noon if you start early in the morning. What do you say?" *Sadananda* looked expectantly at *Govinda*. His suggestion sounded just fine to the *kuanr* who immediately conceded. Opening the front door, they came out to speak to Durga.

Durga Dasa broke into tears at the sight of the *kuanr*. "Your Majesty, the palanquins are ready. At Your Majesty's order, we can start the journey at the earliest auspicious hour," he begged.

"All right, we will come. But not now. I must attend to some work at the college tomorrow morning. After that, I will leave for our village tomorrow evening. *Sadei bhai* will go tomorrow morning."

The *Srikaran* society of *Jhankada* was highly displeased with the irresponsible conduct of both the *kuanr* and *Sadananda*. They could not openly condemn it because they were the zamindar *sa'anta's* own children. *Durga Das* was upset with the indifference with which the *kuanr* received the news of his mother's illness. Determined not to give up he persisted, "Your Majesty, you must not make even the slightest delay if you really intend to catch the last glimpse of Her Majesty. You must leave for the village at this very instant."

"Didn't I say that I will come tomorrow? How many times do you want me to repeat that?" said the *kuanr* curtly. He looked at *Sadananda* who signaled him blinking his eyes. *Govinda Chandra* went inside quickly without waiting to hear *Durga Das's* appeal.

Durga Das was nobody's fool. He guessed that it was something else, not the work at the college that was holding *Govind Chandra* back. He was filled with an apprehension that something very serious might have happened to *maa sa'antani* in the meantime. "I should go back to the village instead of waiting here," he thought. "You all wait here," he told the palanquin bearers. "Tomorrow the *kuanr Sadananda babu* will come to the village in the palanquins."

On their way to the village, *Raghu Bagha Singh* said, "Didn't you see *Abadhane!* How *Sadananda babu* was signaling his brother?"

"Yes, everyone in *Jhankada* knows who has orchestrated the whole design by now. The fellow is still under the blissful impression that everyone thinks he's innocent. It was because our *sa'antani* took mercy on that poor orphan and allowed him an entry in the palace that he is enjoying such privileges. But he is a villain by blood. Will ever a thief's son ever turn out to be a saint? But this is not the time to talk about all that. At present, our biggest concern is *Sa'antani's* health. May the good lord *Sri Gobinda Jiu* keep our *sa'antani* protected under the shadow of the wheel he holds. We will deal with the villain later."

CHAPTER - 29
SIGNING THE LETTER

On reaching the palace of *Sankarshan Mahanty*, the zamindar of *Samsharpur*, *Rajivalochan* went straight to meet his *mamu sa'anta*. As he bent low to bow at his feet *Sankarshan Mahanty* asked, "*Raju*, my child, when did you reach? Why have not you brought them along with you?" He sounded anxious. "You know we have to be very cautious for a few months. The slightest carelessness on our part may bring forth a serious problem.'

"You don't have to worry on account of that *mamu sa'anta*,", said *Rajivlochan* with a smile of confidence. "It is only that we must have a hold on *Sadei bhai*. They will be arriving here next Monday. It is all fixed. Today I will write another letter to them confirming the program."

"My child, do not rest easy and leave everything to *Sadananda*. The fellow is sly and unscrupulous. The need of the time is to keep the man in a stronghold."

Taking leave of his uncle *Rajivlochan* went inside. He made way towards *Indumati*'s room in the inner quarters of the palace. *Indumati* bowed at her brother's feet and stood to lean on the doorpost. *Rajivlochan* too wanted to know from his sister if everything was fine with her.

"Brother *sa'anta*, is everybody else at Cuttack in good health?" asked *Marua*, *Indumati's* maid, and closest companion. Embarrassed at the way *Marua* put the question, *Indumati* cast an angry look at her friend. "Everyone is fine there. *Sadananda bhai, Govind* and I were staying together. The letter from *Mamu Sa'anta* brought me here urgently. They will be arriving here on Monday."

Indumati had quickly gone inside at the mention of *kuanr Govind*'s name. Before he took leave of *Indumati Rajivlochan* stood on the doorway of her bedroom and said, "Dear sister *Indu*, I have something to ask of you. I hope you will not turn my request down."

"Of course, *Raju bhai*, please tell me what it is," said *Indumati* humbly.

"I will tell you in the evening," said *Rajivlochan* and left the room.

After eating his evening meal, *Rajivlochan* sat down to write letters. He wrote two: a long one to *Sadananda* and a relatively short and formal one to *Govind Chandra*. In the second letter, he wrote that everything was fine in the palace and how everybody in the palace was waiting eagerly for him. He sealed both the letters and wrote down the address on each.

After finishing up the letters *Sadanand* started copying down a poem on a sheet of paper. The poem was written in Cuttack. Both *Sadananda* and *Rajivlochan* had jointly written it in consultation with each other. *Govind Chandra* had no knowledge of this. Later in the evening, *Rajivlochan* went to *Indumati* carrying the poem.

"Dear *Indu*, I have never asked you for anything before. But now I have a request to make to you. Please don't say no!" *Rajivlochan* said smiling affectionately.

"Please, *Raju bhai*, do not say such things. You are my elder brother. Your wish is my command. Tell me what it is you want me to do."

"Well, All right. Then please do as I say." He handed her the paper on which the poem was written.

Indumati ran her eyes on the contents, guessed what it was all about and blushed.

"What is this *Raju bhai*?" She asked feigning ignorance.

"Write down your name under the poem," *Rajivlochan* said.

Indumati now realized what all this meant. She trembled inwardly. Her heart raced. She stood speechless for a few moments and put the letter slowly down at *Rajivlochan's* feet.

"No *Indu*! You have to write your name below," he persisted.

Indumati could not speak. Her tongue felt frozen. With much effort, she said in a wet, broken voice, "Please forgive me, brother! This is cheating! I can't take false credit. Do not compel me, I beg of you."

Under the veil that hid her face *Indumati's* eyes were brimming with tears of guilt and self-condemnation but *Rajivlochan* did not notice.

"Why do you say it is false? What is false about it?" *Rajivlochan* asked persuasively.

"I don't have the ability to judge what is true and what is false. But you are my elder brother. You must help guide my morals. But I am sure that my conscience will never permit me to exercise my claim over something that is not my own." *Indu* paused and began to sob holding the border of her sari pressed to her nose.

A man may be treacherous, selfish and impious. But the mention of conscience and morals will surely make him waver. *Rajivlochan*, for reasons similar, could not summon the courage to put pressure on her. He knew by now that *Indumati* would not comply. He was utterly disappointed realizing that her refusal to sign the paper would upset the plan he had worked so meticulously on.

"There is news that some important *karans* from the palace of *Chandanpur* will be coming here to fetch *Govind* to his home. Once he goes to his palace at *Chandanpur* the *srikaranas* of village *Jhankad* will never let him return to Cuttack on one pretext or another. That will spoil everything!!' *Rajivlochan* was terribly disturbed. "What a pity!" He said to himself. "I am going through such efforts to see that she is happily settled! Working day and night without caring for my own comfort! But the foolish girl does not understand that whatever I am doing is for her own good!"

Rajivlochan stood quietly for a moment pondering what he should do in the present situation. An idea struck his conniving mind. "Let me speak to *mamu sa'anta*. The whole game is going to bungle unless he intervenes." He walked slowly to the chamber where the zamindar reclined. The zamindar and his nephew *Rajivlochan* talked in a hushed voice about how to go about the situation. "Well, I will speak to her," said the zamindar after a long discussion. He put his feet into the ivory topped clogs and walked up to *Indumati*'s quarters.

"*Indu*, my child!" he called standing outside his daughter's room. The fond familiar address which used to incite an innocent joy in Indu now filled her with serious misgivings. Had it been some other day she would have hurried out of her room to meet her father. But she could not do so this evening because she had guessed the reason for the untimely presence of her father there. Her feet seemed to have turned to wood. *Marua* hurried to spread out a brocaded carpet on the verandah.

"There is no need for that, I will just have a brief talk

with *Indu*," the zamindar said. He inquired from his daughter about her health and her studies and other topics of small talk. The answers he received from his daughter were mostly monosyllabic and short. "All this is just a way of preparing the ground for what actually he intends to tell me!" *Indu* said to herself and waited for her father to come to the point. In the end, the zamindar *sa'anta* smiling fondly at his daughter said persuasively, "My child, please do as *Raju* says. I would appreciate it if you do so. Do not turn down the request, my dear!" he said and strode away clicking the clogs. *Indu* felt numb. She stood for a long time like a puppet leaning against the doorpost. She felt so lost that the clicking sound of her father's clogs receding away did not reach her ears to tell her that he had left. It was only when *Marua* called out to her that she realized that the father had left the room.

"I cannot disobey father—but how can I lie to my husband, the priceless gem I treasure in my heart, and the ultimate lord of my life? He is more precious to me than my own life—!! Won't my lord be misled to believe that the poem was written by me when he sees my signature under it? What a deplorable deception it will be!!" *Indumati* was caught in a terrible dilemma. She was stuck between her sense of duty to her father and her own better judgment. Her virtue and her better judgment persuaded her to stick to her conscience. *Listen Indu, I am Justice—I hold the world poised in place. I preserve and protect humans from evil. Only I support and sustain the humans in this and the other world.* The next moment her love and her respect for her father overpowered the pleadings of her conscience.

Indu! —Think carefully…

The father is the lord absolute for the child. You are a sensible girl. Just think how indulgent a father he has been!

With what love and commitment he has been rearing you with since the day mother left the world! He used to spend sleepless nights sitting by your bedside when you fell sick. He will go to any lengths and sacrifice anything, even his own blood to protect you and see you live in comfort! He has exhausted all the love of his heart on you and you only! He strives day and night just to see you happy. Could you hurt him by not fulfilling his wish? You know you have never disobeyed him. How can you do that now?

Indumati was startled at the thought of going against her father. "I can't hurt my father," she decided. 'But I must not be false to my husband. I shall have to adopt a middle course that would accomplish both ends. I will write my name below the poem now and tell the truth to my husband and beg his forgiveness falling at his feet when he comes here." Her agitated mind was put to rest after she made her decision.

"Indu!"

Rajivalochan called from the door of her room. The dim lighting in the room had caused *Indumati* not to see him until he called her name. She was slightly startled. *Rajivlochan* handed her a pen and the paper with the poem. He put down the inkpot on the floor. "Use this ink to write your name," he said. *Indu* understood the intent of *bhai sa'anta* but did not speak a word. She did not read the poem before putting her name under it. Quietly, resignedly, she moved close to the lamp, dipped the nib of the pen in the inkpot and wrote her name with a hand that was far from steady. Breathing out a deep sigh she returned the letter to *Rajivlochan*.

CHAPTER - 30
LETTERS DISPATCHED

Relieved and happy, *Rajivlochan* strode back to his own room as soon as *Indumati* returned the signed paper over to him. He had already written the name of *kuanr Govind Chandra* on one of the envelopes. He put the paper and the letter he had written to *Govind Chandra* in that envelope. The zamindar *sa'anta* also had written a letter to his son-in-law. *Rajivlochan* put that one in the same envelope along with the other two. The envelope that contained his letter written in English to *Sadananda* had been sealed already. Now he put all three envelopes in another larger one and sealed it carefully. He gave the big envelope to the pair of post-carriers stationed at the front entrance of the palace. These carriers were posted in pairs at different points of the road that led to Cuttack. Each pair would then take letters to the next checkpoint with carriers and so on. "Look, there are strict orders from uncle *sa'anta*," he warned the first pair. "See that the packet reaches his son-in-law at his residence at *Sheikh Bazar* in Cuttack before dawn tomorrow. All of you post-carriers will be put to task if any negligence is detected. And I will see to it that all of you are fired!!"

CHAPTER - 31

Early next morning in Cuttack, *Sadananda babu* and *kuanr Govind Chandra* sat on the outer verandah of their *Sheikh Bazar* residence, brushing their teeth. Suddenly they noticed a pair of post-carriers hurrying from a distance in their direction. *Sadananda* immediately guessed why this was. "Look, *Sadei bhai*," said the *kuanr*, "how the post-runners are running in this direction. They look familiar...Oh yes, they are *from Samsharpur*, aren't they?"

"We'll let them come a bit closer and then we'll find out," *Sadananda* said, feigning ignorance.

"No, no," said the *kuanr*, "I know them. They are from *Shamsharpur*."

The post-runners finally arrived and bowed and greeted the two young men. They were short of breath as they came running from a distance. They tried to show they were more exhausted than they actually were by gasping harder.

One of the post carriers removed a big envelope from a length of shawl he had wound around his waist and handed it to the elder of the young men who tore it open and took out the smaller envelopes. Holding the envelope addressed to him he handed the others to *Govind Chandra*. The latter opened the letters and began reading them. There was one letter which he read several times and a shy smile danced on his lips every time he did so. This was the poem that *Indumati* had signed on the inciting of *Rajivlochan*.

Lord Vinod Vihari,
The family's tutelary deity
I bow at His feet before I begin;
Accept the respectful greetings
 Of this *dasi* of yours
O my lord, merciful and benign;

At your feet I submit
O' Lord of this life of mine
Please know that here in the palace
Everything is well and fine;

Of your lovely feet to catch a sight
My eyes wait through eager days and nights;

When the college closes you will come
Did not you say?
One measures like a year
As I keep counting each passing day,
What more shall I pray?

The food like poison now tastes
What is there that can sustain me here
O my lord, in your absence?

Do not disappoint me O Lord of my life
Come soon I beg with joined palms
Her heart and mind at your kind feet
Surrenders this maiden ignorant;

May Fate smiled upon me
 So I can serve at your feet soon
What more is there to say?
May I have a glimpse of your benign self
And your blessings too
Your *dasi Indumati* thus does pray.

Sadananda had finished reading his letter. But he held the paper in front of his face pretending to be still reading while he cast furtive glances at *Govind Chandra* out of the corner of his eyes to watch his reaction. The smile on *Govind's* face told him that he had fallen in their trap. *'It has worked!'* he said to himself. Feigning ignorance again, he asked aloud, "Who has written the letter? Must be *Raju bhai,* isn't it? But who has written the other ones?"

"One is from father-in-law and the other — —!" *Govinda* flushed and lowered his eyes.

"What does the zamindar *sa'anta,* your father-in-law say?"

"He wants me to come to *Samsharpur.*"

"*Raju bhai* too mentions that in his letter. Perhaps your presence is urgently needed there for some reason. Haven't I been repeatedly telling you that? I don't think that will be a problem. If you don't feel comfortable there, you can fulfill formalities and leave in the morning. As far as I know, about half a dozen boats are kept moored at the wharf on the riverside by the *cutcherry* hall of the zamindar. The oarsmen are usually ready to enter the boats in the water at any time. I will be arriving at our palace at *Chandanpur* in *taluka Dashagram* in the morning. If you set out early in the morning you will be reaching our village by noon."

"Suits me fine," said *Govinda Chandra.*

Sadananda was elated at *Govind Chandra's* consent to his suggestion.

CHAPTER - 32

Rajanitimirabagunthite puramarge ghanasabda ki klabam
Asati twayee kaminam priyam twa drute prapayeetum kah
eshwarah

In a night draped in darkness and echoing with the
rumbling of clouds

Only the unchaste and the lustful venture outside
and move briskly on

Aspiring for the company of lovers as if they pursue
a path leading to God!!

Sadananda babu was busy most part of Friday night
preparing for *Govind*'s journey to *Samsharpur*. He got the
kuanr ready to go before sunrise the next morning. The
two walked out to the palanquin that was waiting in the
front yard. Old *Nidhi Panigrahi* who had come with them
from the village to cook for them had also come outside
along with them. Keeping a pinch of snuff on his fingertip
he sniffed at it as he watched the palanquins being readied
for the journey. The old man was not just an ordinary,
unlettered cook. He had been with the zamindar since his
childhood looking after the matters relating to zamindari
and had acquired a certain knowledge of different subjects
and gathered enough experience. The man was nobody's
fool. Both the *sa'anta* and the *sa'antani* trusted him a lot.
He was sent to Cuttack to take care of the cooking for both

young men. Both *Sadananda* and *Govinda Chandra* knew that he was one of *sa'anta's* trusted valets and hence they treated him with little deference. That was the reason why *Sadananda* was making all the arrangements without the knowledge of *Nidhi Panigrahi*.

The old man had guessed that it was *Sadananda's* cunning design to send the *kuanr* to *Samsharpur*. But he did not have the courage to raise any objection being a servant. But now the simple, orthodox old man could not contain his disagreement any longer.

"This is not at all a propitious time for a journey because today Saturn casts its evil influence both at the time of sunrise and sunset," he said, hoping that it might dissuade them from traveling to *Samsharpur*. "Besides the stars, *Magha* and *Ashlesha* are currently crossing each other. In addition to that today is the ninth day of the lunar fortnight and on this day the *yogini* or the 'ominous female' is said to be stalking the north direction. Any journey at this crucial period is strictly forbidden."

But the words of the old man made *Sadananda* laugh out loudly. "A bloody fool," he intoned derisively. The *Kuanr*, too, with a facetious smile flickering on his lips, got into the palanquin. The palanquin bearers lifted the palanquin over their shoulders and moved on crying out, "hum, ham…"

"*Sadei bhai*, when shall you start?" asked *Govind Chandra* just before the palanquin started moving. "Just now, I am all ready to go," returned the elder brother. "Listen, all of you,' he called out to the palanquin bearers, "You will receive good tips if you carry the palanquin to the palace before evening."

The barber boy *Saita*, carrying a bundle of his own clothes over his shoulder and a thin towel wound around his head to protect himself from the sun strode behind the palanquin. Nobody bothered about him. Poor boy! He could not help what was happening even though he did not want it to happen. "It will be well into the night by the time *kuanr sa'anta* reaches the palace at *Samsharpur*," he thought to himself. "Of course, some arrangements would have been made for lunch on the way." But he was not too sure about that. So, he went to a streetside snack-shop and bought some snacks and sweetmeats for eight *annas* for the *kuanr*. He also bought some betel leaves and betel-spices for one *anna*. But he did not buy anything for himself. The palanquin arrived at the mango grove at *Gobindpur* around noontime. The palanquin carriers put down the palanquin on the ground and sat down under the shade of the trees. Some of them roamed about in the grove taking off the cloth wound around their waist and began fanning themselves with it. *Saita* looked around to see if there was any arrangement made for cooking but found none. Only a couple of cowherd boys moving about in the grove. Some village urchins driven by curiosity had gathered and watched the palanquin. *Saita* had seen how that on the day of the *kuanr sa'anta's* wedding, several servants arriving from the palace had stood to wait in the grove when the palanquin had reached there. They had made all the cooking arrangements way before the palanquins carrying *Sadananda* and *Govind Chandra* arrived. But today, not a single man from the palace was there. The *kuanr sa'anta* surprised that no one from the palace was there to greet them, stood still like a wooden puppet, thinking. After a long time he spoke out as if remembering something, "A message wasn't sent to the palace about our arriving here today—why should anyone from the palace be present here, waiting?"

He looked wonderingly at his trusted servant *Saita,* and asked, "It is almost noon. What about food?"

"I was also thinking the same thing, *sa'anta,* there seems to be no arrangement made for our midday meal."

"The great *Sadei bhai* is supposed to have looked into everything!" *Saita* thought grudgingly. "He has forgotten about the most important thing!!"

"Your Majesty *kuanr sa'ante,*" he said respectfully looking at the *kuanr.* "Why don't you take a bath in the river? I will see what can be done in the meantime." The *kuanr* knew that *Saita* was a clever boy. He would have made some arrangements. But he did not say anything. *Saita* took out the *kuanr's* bathing towel and handed it to him. "Could I have a little oil to apply on my body before I bathe?" Remembering the situation, they were in the immediately corrected himself — —" Oh, how stupid of me! Where will we get oil here? I will have to do without it."

River *Machhua* flowed by the grove, just a little below ground level. When the *kuanr* came back after taking a bath in the river, he found *Saita* had already served the snacks and sweetmeats on a banana leaf. He had also put a small pot of water by the plate. The *kuanr* looked at *Saita* in surprise for a long moment. "Where did you get all this from?" he asked. "And where is your food?"

"Let Your Highness have something to eat first. I will eat later," *Saita* replied humbly.

The palanquin bearers in the meantime had taken a dip in the water and were wondering what to do about their midday meal. Clever *Saita* knew that the palanquin bearers might do without curry, but they would require at least a seer of cooked rice each for their noontime meal or else they would not be able to lift the palanquin over their shoulders. Taking a couple of palanquin bearers with him he ran to the market of village *Gobindapur* which was about half a mile away from the grove. He bought earthen cooking pots, fire-wood, brown coarse rice and two seers of black gram for the pulses to go with the rice. He bought some beaten rice and treacle for himself and returned.

Kuanr Govind Chandra was prodding the bearers on. He asked them to take the palanquin to the palace before the evening worship of the deity Vinod Vihari began. The cooking, eating and clean up took almost three hours. Though the men worked fast, they could not start before two in the afternoon. But they hurried on. The repeated directives from the *kuanr sa'anta* and the temptation of a covetable tip urged them on. It was after dusk by the time the palanquin reached the ferry-*ghat* at *Sursuria. Bidia Behera,* the ferryman, came running and bowed at the *kuanr's* feet. "Master, it will take some time before you can be ferried across," he said humbly, his palms joined. "There were not many passengers today since it is not the day of the *haat.* So there was no need for the larger boat and the village headman *Makra Padhan* has borrowed it to take his farm laborers across. Master, you can see for yourself how the river is swelling with rainwater. I cannot venture to ferry even three men across the river in this canoe, let alone the palanquin."

"How can the palanquin then be ferried to the other bank?" asked a puzzled *Govind Chandra.*

"Your lordship," said the ferryman, "after the larger boat returns, we will tie both boats together. Then the palanquin can be lowered on to the boats and be carried along."

The *kuanr sa'anta* took out two rupees and gave the money to the boatman *Bidia.* 'Here, take this money. Send a couple of errand boys to the village where the bigger boat is with a message to the village head to send it back as early as possible."

"Your lordship, since the boat will move downstream on its way back, it will not take more than an hour to get back here. It all depends how soon the message carrier reaches village *Bilapada*," assured the boatman.

Trouble never comes alone. The weather was cloudy all day. A few occasional drizzles during the day had made the paths muddy. It was the dark phase of the lunar fortnight and the overcast sky made the evening darker still. The visibility was so poor that you couldn't have seen someone five feet away from you. To make the atmosphere even more dreadful, crooked lightning danced across the sky. Some of the palanquin bearers, who stretched out on the wet ground to relax, now had drifted to sleep. The *kuanr su'anla* was feeling increasingly restless and irritable. He kept on coming out of the palanquin and then going back inside it. He was now thoroughly distraught. When he started for *Samsharpur* in this morning, he was so enthusiastic, full of expectancy. He imagined how he would spend the evening with *Indumati* reading poems and exchanging sweet endearments. He was beginning to feel hungry too. He had nothing else to eat during the long journey except the scanty meal of snacks that *Saita* had brought. When he could not stand it any longer, he called the ferryman and asked him to take him and *Saita* across in the fishing boat to the other side.

"How long will we have to wait for the big boat to return? You better ferry me and *Saita* across to the other side. We would rather sit under the big banyan tree there."

The boatman was not inclined to ferry the *kuanr sa'anta* like any ordinary passenger in the small boat. In the meantime, large rain-swollen clouds had gathered up across the sky. It was going to rain at any moment. Since the palanquin would remain on this side of the river until the big boat came back, the *kuanr sa'anta* would be drenched in looming rain. But how could he refuse the zamindar's son-in-law? He took them both to the other side in the small boat. The master and his valet climbed up to the bank and settled on a thick, sturdy root of a banyan tree.

But the *kuanr* was not able to maintain his calm anymore. He was getting up and sitting down repeatedly. Hunger gnawed at his stomach with all its force. But the glowing face of *Indumati* flashed in the dense darkness from time to time and consoled his aching body and heart to some extent. His gaze traveled frequently towards the dimly visible palace of the zamindar in the distance.

River *Machhua* flowing straight in the northern direction passed the length of the backyard compound wall of the palace and took a turn towards the east. It then snaked along for about nine miles flowing under the land level and crossed the palace bounds of the zamindar of village *Jhankad*. After moving still further for two or three miles it entered river *Mahanadi* at the village of *Bhimpur*. There was a door in the backyard compound that opened straight to the part of the river that served as the bathing *ghat* of the palace.

Kuanr sa'nta glanced across the river constantly. "Hey boatman," he asked impatiently, "when will the big boat get?"

"Not anytime soon master," replied the poor boatman. "Even if it starts without any delay it will be midnight by the time it anchors up here. Otherwise, it can't get here before dawn." The boatman's reply hit the *kuanr* like a bolt of lightning. A deep sigh heaved out of him. He felt as if his frustration would roll down his eyes unless he controlled it with effort. "The palace is less than a mile from here, I can walk instead of just waiting here," he thought. "No, no, how can I walk up to the front entrance of the palace?" He debated with himself. "After all, I am the son-in-law of the zamindar here. Who knows, even at this time some men employed under the zamindar like the almanac-readers, the watch guards, the farm laborers, and errand runners might be sitting in the front yard. Won't it belittle my status if I walk up to them in the darkness? The few days I was here after the wedding, I didn't even go to the bathing *ghat* without a palanquin. His father-in-law had advised him not to go walking anywhere since it would tell upon his social status. Will not the whole village laugh at my back if I walk up a mile in the depth of the night now?" So he dropped the idea. But the urgings of his heart were difficult to ignore. After all, where there is a will there is a way. Suddenly, another idea struck him. He remembered that there was a narrow foot track that went straight through the mango grove to the bathing *ghat*. He had noticed the path during his stay in the palace while he used to saunter by the riverside. He also knew that the window at the backside of *Indu's* bedroom overlooked the river. After taking her evening meal she used to sit in a chair by the window looking at the river until late into the night. He took out the small watch from his pocket and looked at it. It was fifteen minutes after ten. Since no one was permitted to go to the back of the palace the place was always deserted even during the daytime. "It would be really fun if I walked along the narrow path up to her window and surprised her! Her maid *Marua* will stealthily open the door leading to the bathing *ghat* to let me in. When the palanquin arrives at dawn, the entrance will be deserted and I can come out through the backdoor and quickly walk up to the palanquin. Everyone will think that I have just arrived!"

Deciding his move, the *kuanr* tightly wound up his shawl around his waist and set out. "You wait here until the palanquin arrives and come with the palanquin. Caution the bearers not to make any sound while carrying the palanquin to the palace," the *kuanr* advised the barber boy *Saita*. He understood his master's intention. But he was reluctant to let his master venture into this risky journey alone. So, he followed him. "I will come back to wait for the palanquin after I saw you safely reach the palace," he implored.

"No no," said the *kuanr*. "You wait here." Poor *Saita* had no choice other than to obey his master's order. And the *kuanr* keyed himself up to undertake his adventure.

Clusters of black clouds sailed across the pitch-black sky. The mango grove was engulfed in darkness. But the *kuanr* was undeterred. "It is just a mile or so from here. The pathway goes straight to the palace. It won't take much time to cover such a little distance," he thought confidently as he moved on braving the darkness.

But what was this? Where was the path that led to the palace? The *kuanr* had strayed into the woods and had lost his way. The thick growth of weeds had bled into the pathway and had buried it. He moved ahead in the unfamiliar surroundings and encountered the spiky shrubs and bramble bushes that pricked at him constantly scratching him all over. He blindly groped ahead, pushing aside the creepers that had grown into the path entangling it completely. The muslin dhoti and shirt he had worn were now torn at different places. As he sloshed across the muddy, wet grounds water entered his shoes. He moved on wading through the mud and the slush making the water splash about him. He struggled on, his shoes squelching, drenched all over in the muddy water. Rainwater that had settled on the foliages of the trees from the drizzles in the evening dripped down, wetting his head and streaming down his face. But the *kuanr* moved forward careful to keep going straight. He was afraid he might wander in the wrong direction if he turned his face. So, he kept looking straight ahead determinedly. A flock of jackals roamed about searching for food and were disturbed by the human smell and scurried away into the jungle. The *kuanr* strode on. Sometimes a small flame of hope flickering in the heart has enough power to illumine the darkness outside.

CHAPTER - 33

Whatever is wished for slips out of our reach,
While things never expected usually happen —-

It was a big, well-furnished room. Though slightly shabby, it was tastefully decorated with several artifacts. An ornate king-size bedstead that could accommodate four to five people stood against the inner wall of the room. A couple of floral cotton stuffed wool quilts were laid over the mattress and a pair of clean white bedspreads were spread out on them. Soft cylindrical and round pillows were placed on the head and foot of the bed. A mosquito net made of silk with frilly borders hung above the bed. On the bed lay propped a beautiful young woman of about sixteen. Lying in that posture there on that milk-white bed the maiden, with her well-proportioned figure and a complexion like a champak flower, made an impression of some goddess floating in a frothy white pool.

It was past midnight. Another beautiful young woman of about twenty holding a burning candle stood at the doorway. She put out the flame and entered the room. Shutting the door behind her she walked over to the bedstead and peered through the mosquito net. Biting her lower lip mischievously she asked with a smile, "Oh! Our princess is still awake!!"

"No, *Marua*, I don't know why sleep isn't coming

tonight. There is a strange agitation inside me," replied the young woman from the bed.

"True, True," said *Marua* smiling. "It is natural for you to feel restless. You need to be patient for a few more days. On the night after next, by this time, another moon will have made its appearance on this bed. And now you should go to sleep—-"

"Oh go away!" returned the young woman who lay on the bed. "I will break into tears if you speak like that once again. God knows why I have been disturbed all day. Nothing interests me."

"How come?"

"No idea. I feel like crying. A strange fear seems to have taken me in its grip."

"What is there to fear princess? The palace is guarded by sentries on all sides. It is the house of the lord of the village. Which burglar or thief has the mettle to dare a heist here?"

"Didn't dacoits make a forced entry into *Ghana Mahanty's* house the other night? They broke open his door with crowbars and swept the house clean of all valuables. Have you closed the window of our room properly?"

"Look there, how strongly I have bolted it," assured *Marua*.

Just as she pointed at the window on the far side of the room, a soft knock came from the backyard door of the palace. A startled *Marua* gaped at the window, unable to decide the sound had come from.

The knocking grew louder. As *Marua* turned to face the younger woman, her mouth opened in terror and the later jumped out of the bed screaming. Both girls grabbed each other tightly and shouted at the top of their voice,

"Help, Help—the dacoits are here!!" The soft knock now had turned to loud, hard beating and a voice spoke amidst the screams of the two maidens— 'Quiet, Quiet, there are no dacoits. It is me!" The two young women could not hear the voice. But they mistook the beating for something else. "The dacoits are breaking the window with crowbars!" The young women, all their energy exhausted, grew too scared to speak. Only a low grunting sound escaped them. Soon they fell on the floor and collapsed.

Some of the tenants in the servant quarters of the ladies' wing of the palace had gone to sleep spreading out mattresses on the floor. Some were cleaning utensils after having their supper while some were still eating. When they heard the commotion, they ran into their rooms and bolted the door without waiting to see what exactly had happened and began screaming wildly. The zamindar *sa'anta* was preparing to go to sleep on the cot that stood in the cutchery hall. He no longer slept in his bedroom after the death of his wife. The loud noise from the ladies' quarters had reached his ears now. He took out a sword from the scabbard that hung against the wall and strode into the inner section of his palace. Four night-watchmen who stood guard in the cutchery premises ran after him each carrying a staff. "What is the matter?" the *sa'anta* asked loudly. But who would answer? The servant maids were howling like crazy. No one had ears for the *sa'anta's* question. Exasperated beyond control, the *sa'anta* kicked hard at one of the doors of a room. A loud scream, "Help help, the dacoit is breaking in——-" was heard from behind the door and then there was silence. The maid, in all probability, had lost consciousness.

Without waiting to ask anybody anything the *sa'anta* went around the palace along with the night guards, one of whom held a flaming torch. After a thorough search, he arrived at the decision that no dacoit had entered the palace. The sentries filling the air with their triumphant cries moved around the palace. Below the compound wall on the right side, four guards sat around a burning campfire. Their swords were held in scabbards hung on the walls. The four kept a vigil watch on the palace in turns divided into four phases. The *paika* who supervised the safeguarding of the palace during that phase of the night stood sword in hand and shouted warnings from time to time.

Galvanized into action at the noise in the palace, all four guards rushed towards it, swords and cudgels in hand. Since the commotion was first heard from the room of the zamindar's daughter they ran along the length of the compound wall in that direction. The *paikas* was an ancient warrior class of Odisha. Now that the clan had lost its ancient glory, what remained behind were only their swords, a legacy of their gallant forefathers, and the courage to plunge into an adventure without a second thought. Of late, most of the *paikas* were fast losing that bravery while the rest were following suit.

On the riverside, a flock of jackals was scooping out small crabs from the sand. Startled at the loud screams of the *paika* guards they ran blindly for their lives. A few, in utter fear, jumped into the river and swam to the other side. In the pitch darkness the guards, judging by the sound of the loud splash caused as they jumped into the water, mistook them for the dacoits and ran after them blindly. Scared, the jackals ran for their lives at great speed. Suddenly lightning flashed across the sky. The *paika* guards saw a figure in white standing below the window of the zamindar's daughter. "Look there stands one of them!" shouted one *paika* and in the next instant, all eyes turned towards the white figure. All four guards ran towards the man in white. The figure seeing the guards heading in his direction blundered into the jungle. But he could not run far. His foot got caught in the wet dhoti he wore, and he fell with a crash losing his balance. But the *paikas* had no trouble moving quickly through the spiky shrubs in the jungle. They were on him within a second and grabbed him. All at once, they landed hard blows and slaps on him as he lay defenseless and immobile. One of the *paika* guards pulled both his hands behind his body and tied them together tightly with a length of cloth he wrenched out from his waist. The dacoit offered no resistance. The guards saw that he had lost consciousness.

"The man looks like a *babu*," some of them said. "Let's not beat him anymore. There will be trouble if he dies. Better take him to the zamindar *sa'anta.*' Holding him by his arms they tried to make the man stand up. But it was of no use since the man had lost consciousness. Two *paika* guards lifted him over their shoulders carried him like a dead body. Swelling in pride at their bravado they took him to the *cutchery* hall and tied him to a pillar. A constable, *Bandidin Mishra*, deployed by the *sadar* police station to keep guard at the palace, was lying in a deep slumber on a charpoy in the verandah of the *cutchery* hall. The loud cries of the *paika* guards woke him up. He stroked his beard proudly, as though the credit was all his, and readily took the dacoit into custody. Putting the dacoit in the constable's charge the *paika* guards went away to resume the chase of the other dacoits that might have gotten away. They came across the *sa'anta* at the back of the palace. The *paikas* smacked their biceps and stamped their feet on the ground. Then they touched their sword point to the ground and to their foreheads to offer battle-salutations to their master and spoke at once, "Your Highness, we all pushed into the gang of the dacoits risking our lives — all of them were strong and sturdy men and carried heavy cudgels."

"Your Majesty!" broke in *paika Bhima Paida*, "I saw in the brief flash of the lightning that four of them carried shotguns over their shoulders. But as we pushed through them brandishing our swords all of them ran helter-skelter. Some even jumped into the river and swam away. I alone could have grabbed four or five of them, but they escaped taking advantage of the darkness."

The womenfolk in villages have amusing sayings on such exaggerated boasting of the *paikas*.

At the order of the zamindar, ten flaming torches were brought from the palace. The zamindar himself, along with the *paikas* set out to track the dacoits. They pushed aside the branches and creepers and peered into the darkness. They even looked inside the shrubs and thickets but could not find any trace of a dacoit. "Look carefully," ordered the *sa'anta*, "Follow the footprints!" But after a thorough search, they could not find a single human footprint. Only fresh footprints of some jackals on the wet earth. Coming around the palace they suddenly discovered a single polished black shoe lying under the window of the zamindar-daughter's bedroom. It looked expensive and was of foreign make. One of the guards picked up the shoe and then all of them went inside the palace. The zamindar was tired and had no patience to look at the thief who lay huddled in the *cutchery* hall, tied to a pillar. The zamindar was very upset. As he made way to the indoors, he cast an angry look at the guards and said, "Look at the audacity of these thieves! What will happen to the ordinary households if they dared to break into *my* palace! Under such strict vigil! All right, I will see that their entire dacoit gang is finished!"

The morning star had come up in the east. There was a little time left for daybreak. The empty palanquin carried by the bearers approached the palace door. *Saita* walked in front of the palanquin while two other bearers brought up the rear. The carriers put down the palanquin in front of the main entrance of the palace. The *kuanr sa'anta* must be asleep at this time, *Saita* guessed and waited for the night to end. A group of people sitting on the verandah of the *cutchery* hall talked about the burglary. Curious, *Saita* went up to them to know more about the incident. One of them pointed at the white-clad man tied to the pillar in the middle of the hall. The flame of the lamp had dimmed since the oil in the lamp had burnt away during the night. *Saita* was not able to see clearly in that feeble light. He walked a bit closer to the thief. Now that the lamp was behind *Saita*, his shadow fell on the thief concealing his face. The barber boy kicked hard on the thief's back. "You scoundrel! How dare you steal from our *sa'anta's* place!"

"Oh, oh! Help —-*Saita*!" moaned the thief.

Saita froze. The voice sounded familiar. He pushed the wick in the lamp up a little and peered at the thief. He could not see the face but there was no mistaking the red-bordered dhoti. He himself had helped the *kuanr sa'anta* wear that dhoti yesterday morning. It was torn at several places and soiled with mud. The silk shirt he wore was also in shreds. *Saita* recognized the shoe. It was the one from that expensive pair that had come in a parcel from a footwear store in Calcutta. There was only one shoe, the other foot was bare. It took *Saita* a single glance to figure out who this was. "O God in Heaven! What a terrible thing!" he cried aloud and rushed to unfasten the rope that held the man fixed to the pillar. The constable *Misharji* was loitering about the front yard, elated at the achievement. He shouted to

Saita when he saw the latter untying the thief. "Hey *Bhaiya*, don't let that villain go free. I have captured him. This will get me a promotion. I will be promoted to the post of the *jamadar!*" Who cared about *Mishraji's* promotion? Without paying the slightest heed to the constable's pleadings, *Saita* kept at the task of unfastening the rope, weeping piteously.

"Take me quickly into the palanquin and ask the bearers to carry it to the Cuttack hospital. I may not survive any delay— —." With much effort, the *kuanr sa'anta* could manage to blurt out just these few words to his trusted servant. He lost consciousness in the next instant. *Saita*, helpless tears streaming down his face gathered the unconscious young man in his arms and laid him down carefully in the palanquin. Not able to contain himself anymore he began to wail loudly.

By the time it was morning, a large crowd had gathered in the front yard of the zamindar's *cutcherry*. "The son-in-law of the zamindar *sa'anta* was mistaken for a dacoit and was beaten hard. He was even kept tied to a pillar!" Everyone in the palace was shocked beyond belief as the news reached them. There was a great hue and a cry. *Indumati* did not cry. She only fainted from time to time and the grief-stricken maids kept sprinkling water on her face. *Marua*, was in a state of shock herself. The zamindar *sa'anta*, a patient and strong-willed person himself, was thoroughly distraught. Copious tears ran down his eyes. He was so woebegone that speech deserted him. Half a dozen astrologers and almanac-readers sat by him. They tried in vain to console him. Another half a dozen or so barber-boys, though exhausted by the labor, kept on fanning him.

The clerks of the zamindar's *cutchery* tried to inquire into the matter. But who could tell what exactly had happened? Nobody knew the exact details. The only person who was supposed to have some idea was not in her senses. *Marua* was in no state of recounting the incident. She just looked on blankly, speechless. The truth, therefore, remained buried in the dark.

The zamindar *sa'anta* sat like a wooden puppet, motionless, his vacant gaze fixed at some invisible point above. No one dared to ask him anything.

Poor *Saita* had begged everyone who went inside the palace to pass a word to *Rajivlochan*, but there was no sign of him. Nor did he send a word back to the barber-boy. So weeping pitiably, he begged with folded palms the people who were entering the main door of the palace to inform the zamindar *sa'anta* about the *kuanr*'s serious condition. He begged them to ask the zamindar to have the *kuanr* be carried to the Cuttack hospital. A mere servant as he was, *Saita* did not have the pluck to make a decision on his own.

The clerks brought the urgings of *Saita* to the notice of the zamindar. But the zamindar's mind seemed to register nothing. The astrologers and the clerks were worried about the zamindar's son-in-law. "He is in urgent need of medical attention," they said. "It is not possible to get him proper treatment here in these rural surroundings. He must be transferred to Cuttack."

At last the chief astrologer of the palace, *Binod Mahanty* managed to muster the courage to speak loudly to the zamindar. After some effort, the impact seemed to sink in and the zamindar looked up at the astrologer. "Umm! Umm! Why should he be taken to Cuttack? Send people to call in the best doctors at Cuttack whatever that may cost. Let the treatment be carried on here." *Rajivlochan*, who had been sitting beside his uncle, intervened here, "Your Majesty must think carefully before taking any action.

There is no point in crying over spilled milk. Now we must wisely plan out things. Aren't his family and our family at loggerheads with each other? God forbid if something happens to the *kuanr* here it will lead to a crisis. Why complicate the matter by involving ourselves in it? We are not sending him away from here. But why should we stop him if he wants it that way? No one can blame us if he goes to Cuttack and gets himself medical attention. We can evade all responsibilities by emphasizing our ignorance about everything." Some clerks and astrologers present there approved of *Rajivlochan*'s suggestion. "Young though he is, he speaks wisely," they remarked.

Saita by this time had understood that he would not be receiving any clear instructions from either the zamindar or any of his people. He decided he would get his master transferred to a hospital in Cuttack. Offering a silent prayer to the tutelary deity *Gobindajiu* he called the palanquin bearers to lift the palanquin and proceed. The palanquin bearers had come all the way with an expectation of getting a sumptuous meal at the palace and a handsome wage along with a generous tip. Their hopes belied, they were in a sultry mood. "Brother, you might kill us if you so like, but we do not have a grain of energy left in us to carry the palanquin all the way back to Cuttack," they said.

Barber-boy *Saita* had read the mind of the palanquin bearers. He had carried a pouch tucked under the waist fold of the dhoti he wore. He removed the pouch and took out several coins from it. Without bothering to count he slipped them into the hands of the palanquin carriers. "Lift the palanquin now," he said. "You can stop at the mango grove at *Gobindpur* and cook a good meal for yourselves."

Money has a strange, mysterious power. Once tucked in the waist-fold, it can send electric waves running through the body of the owner making him feel doubly charged with vigor.

Lifting the palanquin over their shoulders the bearers strutted on at a quick pace and arrived at the mango grove in village *Gobindpur* much before midday. They put down the palanquin and began drying their sweating bodies with the cloths they wound around their waists. "Brother, we are drained," they said to *Saita*. "We must have a good meal now. We can't move a step ahead otherwise." *Saita* knew that. So, he took out two rupees from the pouch under his waist-fold and walked to the village to get provisions with two of the bearers. But before that, he had taken good care of his young master. He had carefully taken off the torn clothes and after giving him a light sponging, put him in new clothes. He had cleaned the wounds with a piece of clean cloth which he had torn away from a new dhoti and bandaged them neatly.

The village of *Gobindpur* lay not less than half a mile away from the grove. The village did not have a regular grocery shop. A fellow called *Ram Naik* kept the grocery ready for the wayfarers in case they needed it. The villagers also bought rice, pulses, spices and other things from *Ram Naik*. *Saita* bought the grocery and other cooking essentials from *Ram Naik*. He also inquired where he could get some milk for his master. "I have a milch cow," said *Naik*, but we only milk it in the afternoons. Milking it at this hour will not yield a good quantity." But *Saita* needed the milk urgently. "It does not matter if it's just a little bit. But I must have the milk now. I am ready to pay whatever price you demand."

"Okay, let me see what I can do," said the shrewd shopkeeper and went inside.

Saita, unaware of the fellow's malicious intentions, sat

waiting on the outer verandah of his house listening to the purr of the milk-jets. Eventually, the sound stopped. *Saita* understood that the milking was over. "O' shopkeeper," he called out urgently, "Please get me the milk quickly. I am ready to pay you eight *annas* a seer."

Ram Naik, who was coming out of the house, stopped and looked into the pot. It contained less than half a seer of milk. He went back inside and put the milk pot in a rope-rack hanging from the thatch. "The man is desperate," he thought greedily, "I must squeeze eight annas out of him."

"No, *babu*," he said coming out, "the cow did not allow to milk her—didn't I tell you it was not the proper time for milking? The animal has gone berserk. It may not give milk even at the usual time. It all happened because of you."

Saita was on the brink of tears. "How is the master going to survive without milk?" He stood up and holding the hands of *Naik*, begged, "Brother, you must help me. Try to get some milk for me from anywhere. Here, take this eight *anna* coin. Do not bother even if the milk measures less than a seer." He pushed an eight-*anna* coin into his hand. *Naik* examined both sides of the coin flipping it on his palm. "Not a fake one," he thought to himself. Happy at the profit, he said a little politely, "Master, please wait here. Milk is usually available at *Ram Barik*'s house. I will go to his house and get some. Don't you worry! I will get the milk from anywhere." He went inside and slammed the door shut. "If I get him the milk quickly, he might think I had it here in my home and haggle the cost." So, he sat down on the backyard verandah, rolled in some tobacco leaves and lit it. Putting the tobacco roll between his lips he sat relaxed inhaling the delicious smoke. After a long wait, *Saita* called out his name from the front verandah. "Hey, brother shopkeeper, please hurry." The impatience and urgency in his voice, at last, made some impact on the shopkeeper's deceitful mind. "He should not be kept waiting any longer," he thought and replied from behind the door in a breathless voice, "Just a moment master, I have just come in through the backdoor. I have looked in the whole village and finally managed to get some milk for you."

"Make it quick, I cannot wait any longer." *Naik* took out the milk-pot from the rope-rack and looked inside. The milk wouldn't measure even half a seer. He added an equal amount of water to it and looked again. Satisfied, he opened the front door and came out holding the earthen milk-pot. He breathed in short gasps to give the impression that he was running about from house to house in search of milk. "You are a nice person and it is only because of that that I went from house to house asking for some milk. After a long search, I finally got the milk in *Bhima Paida*'s house. I have come running all the way lest you might be late."

"Give me the milk quickly," said *Saita*, putting out an eager hand. "Where is the container?" asked *Rama Naik*

"I don't have one. Couldn't you give me this pot?"

"How can I give it to you? I collect milk from the cows in this pot."

"Brother shopkeeper," *Saita* said desperately, "I beg of you, let me have it."

Ram Naik's heart softened. "All right, you take this one. Aren't you camping at the mango grove? I will get it back from you in a bit."

Holding the milk-pot carefully on his left palm, it's top covered with the right palm *Saita* ran towards the grove.

CHAPTER - 34
GOSSIPS OVER THE THEFT

Bad odor and sensational news spread through the air very quickly. By noon the subject of the burglary in the zamindar's palace had reached the nook and corners of *taluka Samsharpur*. The gossip traveled from one mouth to other acquiring new dimensions and new shapes. Garrulous persons and tall talkers who possess a rare skill of blowing things out of proportion are everywhere. They are proficient in the art of making any new issue extremely palatable through exaggeration. Almost everyone in the *taluka* had now come to believe that the zamindar's son-in-law had been masterminding all the burglaries which had taken place in the villages.

Some of the sturdy, muscular palanquin bearers lay resting in the front yard of the zamindar's *cutchery* stretching out their tired bodies on cloths they had tied to their waists. People guessed them to be the associates of the zamindar's son-in-law, the real orchestrator of the burglaries. A few gossips decided that there were several gangs of dacoits who operated under the instructions of the zamindar's son-in-law. He planned and organized all these activities sitting in Cuttack. Some subjects in the villages situated on the borders of the *taluka*s of Samsharpur and *Dashgram* who were sent to jail with the insinuations of the zamindar

Baishnaba Charan Patnaik, the *kuanr's* father, had been nursing a grudge against him. Unable to retaliate since the zamindar was beyond the reach of their vengeance they lay curled up and inactive like charmed snakes in the baskets. They were having a heyday now. Delighted that their wrongdoer had received the due return they kept on relating the subject to the people of *taluka Jhankada* adding their own comments to it. "What a shame!! The son of a man of such high status!! So rich and so highly educated! Imagine him forming dacoit-gangs and indulging in the act of burglary!"

"But how long sin will go unpunished?" they added. "Justice had been finally meted out. Now the chief of the gang is put under handcuffs and so are the other members of his gang. The Magistrate Sahib himself had come to the village with about a hundred and fifty constables. The stolen valuables were recovered. They have also gathered enough incriminating evidence to send the zamindar's son to a penal colony. What a relief! The entire *taluka* was spending sleepless nights for fear of these dacoits. People will enjoy sound sleep now."

CHAPTER - 35
INDUMATI

Four days had passed after that eventful night. Since then, *Indumati* had bounced in and out of consciousness. She lay in her bed unaware of her immediate surroundings, her eyes closed. Sometimes she passed on to a state of delirium. Though all her maids kept waiting upon her day and night in turns, *Marua* did not budge from the room. She had forgotten her hunger and sleep and sat by *Indumati's* bed holding a small palm-leaf fan with which she fanned the emaciated figure from time to time. She had been managing to make the girl swallow a few spoonfuls of milk each day with much effort. Most of the milk flowed down from both sides of her mouth. *Indumati's* mind was as empty as her body was motionless.

On the fourth night of the *kuanr sa'anta's* departure, *Indumati* had had a strange dream. Settled on a bejeweled throne studded with coruscating gems set against a clear sky illumined with the silvery brilliance of a thousand moons, was her mother. She was adorned with priceless jewelry and garlands of heavenly flowers. Her face shone with a serene, celestial glow. She appeared to have extended her loving hands towards her daughter as if signaling her. *Indumati's* gaze remained fixed on the dazzling figure. The night was fading as her mother started to speak to her.

"*Indu*, be prepared. This complex, selfish and sinful world is no longer a fit dwelling for you. Recollect the moral instructions that have shaped your approach to life from its very beginning. Death is preferable to dishonoring truth. You may have been prompted by some weakness in your mind to commit an offense. But that also requires atonement."

The ringing of bells and gongs in the temple of Lord *Binod Bihari* jerked *Indumati* to dazed wakefulness. She felt as if a soft radiance emanating from the dazzling image flooded over her and spread inside her, mingling in the blood that ran in her veins. She suddenly sat up on the bed. Since the day the *kuanr sa'anta* had left she was had not been able to get up without the assistance of at least two maids. But on that day, she brushed her teeth and washed without anyone's help. Following the advice of her mother, *Indumati* had made it a routine to pray and then read *The Srimad Bhagavad Gita* every morning. That day after taking her morning bath, she wore a silk sari and adorned herself with the jewelry her mother had given her. She went into the small anteroom that was used as her mother's prayer and worship room and sat there, her eyes closed in prayer. She sat in a trance gazing fixedly at the luminous image of her mother that flashed before her closed eyes. She joined her hands together and prayed to her, "O mother! You have brought me to this earth, and you have taught me how to live my life! You have always advised me to follow the path of truth and righteousness. You have left for your heavenly abode by the cruel decrees of destiny depriving me of your blissful company. But you know, and the omniscient God stands witness to it, that I have never strayed from the path of truth. Nor has any depraved thought ever entered my mind. Oh! How I long for your company! Your absence in my life has landed me in serious trouble. Take me back to your lap my goddess! I have disobeyed you and behaved in an irresponsible manner. Inadvertently though! Now I stand before you as a liar, a sinner and a violator of truth. I have committed a crime spurred on by a momentary weakness. I do not know what sort of penance will absolve it!! I am prepared to bear any form of punishment meted out to me for my misconduct. I would not complain if a thousand lightning bolts blighted me! But I am contemplating the ultimate form of penance."

"Alas! Shame on me! My husband, the crown of my head, the anchor of my life, a man who doesn't even have a slight blemish in his character is passing through a difficult time because he had believed the letter to be written by me. He had abandoned his family, slighted its reputation on account of a wretch like me! He had given up his inheritance to a huge property. But what did *I* do for him? Ungrateful as I am, I had besmeared his clean, flawless character. A delicate body unable to bear the pain of a flower thrown upon it is now suffering from the cruel wounds I have inflicted on it. Alas! Oh! Alas!"

She could not bring herself to think about her husband anymore. She was afraid to imagine where he was and in what condition. But she had had an intuitive feeling that there was nothing wrong with him or else her own heart would have been instinctively torn asunder by its impact. She had often heard her mother saying that chaste women never suffer from the throes of widowhood. "I have never contemplated any offensive deed let alone commit it. Still, I have done something very wrong which demands a difficult penance."

"Alas! How unfortunate I am! I should have nursed the lord of my life, but I do not have even the scope to catch a distant glimpse of him! All right then, I will practice austere penance keeping my heart at his feet."

CHAPTER - 36
DESPAIR

Most of the Hindu philosophical and religious texts preach pessimism as the fundamental principle of human existence. Sage *Gautam* says that humans suffer the pain of birth and the agony of death. The entire lifespan of a human being is a tale of sorrow and woe. Whatever human beings construe as happiness is nothing but a shadow of sorrow. Perhaps the Supreme Creator has been quite parsimonious in allotting happiness in a human being's destiny.

But He had given a man a rare and beautiful gift called 'hope'. One might see it as something promising while another may call it an illusion but hope always motivates a man with its positivity. No one can say how humans would have survived the lows and highs of time had the Supreme Artist not sent 'hope' down to this earth to anchor their life. A person lying in a sickbed experiencing excruciating pain feels that death only could bring him relief. When hope enters his world of dark despair, the suffering man thinks that the sickness and the pain are not permanent and that he will live a healthy and happy life once he recovers. He is spurred by a desire to live on. Hope tells the lamenting mother that has just lost her son, "Why do you mourn? Get up. You can still beget another son!" And the woebegone mother gets up to engage herself in her worldly duties.

The separation from her mother who had been a source of heavenly joy, who had taught her lessons on truth and who had brought her up with great love and care, had rendered *Indumati* heartbroken. Crushed under that huge heap of pain she lay confined to her bed for many days. Slowly but surely, chunks of that huge heap were washed away by the interminable currents of time and hope finally made its way to her grief-stricken heart. 'You should get up now and hold on to your patience,' said hope, 'Your mother was never meant to be with you forever. She had, as it was ordained by destiny, left for the other world having completed her duty of rearing you with love and care. That is the inevitability of our existence. But you must perform your own duties now. Every woman in this world is assigned with certain responsibilities she must discharge with sincerity. Push aside the thick mist of darkness and look. An angel is coming. You will have to do your duties as a woman with his love and support. That hour of bliss is almost here. Get up and wait to receive the ultimate support, the lord of your life."

The sole sustainer woman, whose presence in her life spells fortune and happiness, the living lord of her life did arrive eventually. He was an angel indeed! He hailed from a noble family and had a regal status. He was handsome and well built as Lord *Kartikeya*. People who have a poetic streak in their character, as well as those who do not understand poetry will agree unanimously that he possessed all the good qualities expected in a young man. The ultimate reward of all her virtues accumulated through many lives had finally appeared taking the form of an angel-like human. But as the sun of joy was about to rise, the skyline darkened with thick patches of black clouds and the storm broke out. Thousands of thunderbolts struck her life at once and completely devastated her. She believed herself to be at the root of all this mishap that befell her. And that sense of guilt had killed her will to live.

CHAPTER - 37
INDUMATI

Indumati wandered about the palace silently, her face emptied of all expression. She moved into the garden and looked at the bushes of jasmine, and other fragrant blossoms which she and *Marua* had planted in neat rows. Every afternoon they used to carry water from the river in small brass pots and watered the plants with much care. That day too, *Marua* kept her company while she watered the plants. But she did not smile or chatted with her friend as she had before. She moved like in automaton, from plant to plant. *Marua*, confused at the sudden change that had come over her dear and beloved friend, kept a close watch over her activities. But she was unable to read her mind from her face. *Indu* did not look happy, nor did she look unhappy. She looked dissociated. When *Marua* asked her anything she answered her only in monosyllables.

Others in the palace were happy to see *Indumati* coming out of the confinement of her bedroom. They thought that she had gotten over her sorrow since she no longer wept or sit gloomily holding her head down. Her face held a serious but calm look like a sky before a massive storm. Strangers might interpret such a supine look as the absence of all grief, but not *Marua*. She was terribly disturbed at the changes in *Indumati*. Her mother, Her Majesty *maa*

Sa'antani, while alive, had gotten several sets of gem-studded gold ornaments made for her daughter. She also used to buy them from the jewelry shop owners readymade. It's her passion to acquire different jewelry for her beloved daughter. After all, she was her only child! The jewelry was treasured in the jewelry boxes in a trunk. *Indumati* took out the boxes of ornaments and put them on without thinking. But her mind was elsewhere. Anyone watching her closely would have realized that she was putting them on without any interest. Her face was like a blank sheet.

The palace housed about sixty maids of all ages. She went to all of them one by one and gifted them her jewelry. She gave one a bracelet, another a bangle, a ring to someone else and so on. She walked gingerly towards another young maid called *Nima*, someone she hadn't conversed with at least a year. It had so happened that one afternoon last summer *Indumati* had asked *Nima* to water the flowering plants and went away to her room along with *Marua* to read a book. When she came to the garden in the evening, she found that the plants had not been watered. She had become very upset and was unusually harsh with the girl. "Getaway— Why don't you drop dead?" she had said in a spate of anger. After some time, when she regained her calm, she had repented for her behavior. She was filled with a sense of guilt and was not able to sleep through the night. She was so embarrassed that she had not spoken to the maid since that day. Now she walked up to her and taking off a gold necklace she slipped it around her neck. "*Nima*, I had scolded you that day. Please do not take it to heart and forgive me," she said tenderly. Poor *Nima* fell at her young mistress's feet and wept loudly. "Your Majesty! Why do you speak like this?" Holding her by her arm *Indumati* raised *Nima* up and wiped her tears with the border of her own silk sari.

The news of *Indumati* gifting her jewelry to the maids reached the zamindar *sa'anta*'s ear. "All right let her do what she likes. It is all well and good if her mind is otherwise occupied." Everybody in the palace was relieved except *Marua*. She stole quick glances at Indumati's face from time to time trying to read her mind, but the latter's expressionless face gave her no clue. On other days *Indumati* shared all her secrets with *Marua* but now she seemed totally aloof, dissociated. But as far as *Marua* was concerned such a demeanor was not normal. Several times she braced herself to ask what the matter was but had held it back. *Marua* experienced some unknown fear, something uncanny which she felt in her senses but could not define. She continued to keep a close, protective watch over her mistress and friend.

CHAPTER - 38
MARUA

Bhimsen Malla was the ancestral tenure holder of six *mouzas* of taluka *Samsharpur.* He was a trusted and close associate of the zamindar *Sankarshan Mahanty.* A man of affluence with a reasonable size of the zamindar's property, *Malla* was a pious and benevolent man and was held in esteem by the people of the village. Though his house was always crowded with laborers, maids, domestic help and errand boys, he only had one family member in the form of his motherless four-year-old daughter. Her name was *Marua.*

Cold and flu season started from the middle of the month of *Ashwin* to the end of the month of *Kartika* every year. People routinely suffered from coughs, colds, and fevers in the villages. But that year the disease took a fatal form. It took a toll on many lives in the villages of *taluka Samsharpur. Bhimsen Malla* had come under the clutches of the deadly disease. He lay in bed down with a fever and cough for eight days. A couple of *Vaidyas* attended to him in turns, trying different herbal cures. The zamindar *Sankarshan Mahanty* came in the mornings and evenings to supervise the treatment. On the evening of the ninth day, *Bhimden Malla* expressed his wish to talk to the zamindar privately. He asked everyone else to leave the bedroom. "Your Majesty," he said when they were alone in the room. "I leave my daughter *Marua* in your charge. Kindly take care of the orphan girl. I leave all my property in your hands. Give her hand in marriage to a suitable person when she comes of age." His voice trailed off as he breathed his last breath.

The zamindar had then brought the little girl to the palace and put her in his wife's lap. It was the twenty-first day of *Indumati's* birth. *Marua's* arrival had heightened the mood of the celebration. The little girl wailed calling out for her father. The kind *sa'antani* tried to coax her with sweetmeats and toys. She showered such guileless affection on the girl that *Marua* forgot her father in less than a year. She entertained her kind foster mother with her innocent prattles. "Who are you?" she would lisp and the kind *sa'antani* would answer with a benign smile, "Don't you know? I am your mother!"

"Gopal has a mother. *Chandali* has one too. But my mother died and my father wept."

–"Yes, I had died but now I have come back to you."

"Ok but don't die again. I will cry. Where is my father?"

"He has died too. But he will come back as I did."

Indumati and *Marua* spent the days in each other's company. They played together, ate together, and even slept in one bed. The maids in the palace addressed *Marua* as the elder princess and waited upon her with equal submission as they did *Indumati.* She addressed *Marua* as *apa,* but as she grew up *Marua* realized her position. She became submissive and humble. But neither the kind *sa'antani* nor *Indumati* ever treated her like she was not a part of the family.

After *Bhimsen Malla* succumbed to the fatal fever the zamindar *Sa'anta* sold all his assets and deposited the money in *Marua's* name. He had never touched that money. The principal and the interest put together would now have been about fifty thousand rupees.

The zamindar was on the lookout for an educated, intelligent boy of *khandayat* caste for *Marua*. Though such candidates were available, no one wanted to marry *Marua* on the condition that he would have to live in the palace along with his wife. The zamindar was getting tired of the search. It seemed like the perfect match for *Marua* did not exist. And *Marua* still remained unwed.

CHAPTER - 39
A MOON CALLED *INDUMATI* SANK

She spent the morning along with the maids, speaking to them and giving away gifts of her ornaments to them. In the afternoon she and *Marua* carried water from the river and watered the plants. *Indumati* watered each individual plant. She stood by each plant for some time caressing its leaves fondly. As they went about the act of carrying water from the river in pots and watering the plants in silence *Marua* guessed that something was not normal in *Indumati's* behavior. She kept on glancing at her from the corners of her eyes trying to observe her more closely. She saw that *Indumati* looking intently at the river several times, but she could not guess why. A group of maids stood at a distance watching them watering the plants. A couple of maids had volunteered to fetch water from the river but *Indumati* cast a stern look at them and they fled. So, they stood there silently, scared to come closer.

By the time they were done watering the plants, the mellowing sunlight was receding from the leaves of the trees. It was time to prepare for the evening worship at the temple of Lord *Binod Bihari*. Some maids were engaged in putting ghee and wicks in the prayer lamps. As *Indumati* had expressed her wish to witness the evening worship in the temple, the door-keeper of the temple, old *Mukund*

Barik, hurried to the temple to wash and cleanse the premises. Both *Marua* and *Indumati* went to the river and washed their hands and feet to get ready. Clad in new silk white saris they walked to the temple to offer evening prayers.

After the worship was over the head priest puffed out the flames of two burning wicks and handed each of them the prayer lamps. Both the girls smelled the faint smoke emitting from the wicks with reverence. *Indumati* lay prostrate on the floor and prayed for a long time.

Marua and *Indumati* ate their evening meal at their usual time. *Marua* observed that *Indumati* just nibbled at her food. She got up abruptly without eating half of what was on her plate. *Marua* did not find the energy to coax her to a few more helpings. She too got up, her food half-finished and followed *Indumati* to the bedroom.

They lay down on the same bedstead as they did every night. But on all other nights, they talked for a long time before falling asleep. Their talks centered around the books they read, the flower they had planted, and the happenings at the palace. But that night, neither of them spoke a word, each absorbed in her own thoughts. Time and again they stole surreptitious glances at each other as if one was keeping watch over the other. They lay on the bed, eyes shut, pretending as if they were asleep. But neither of them slept, each stealing quick, cautious glances at the other to ascertain that she had fallen asleep.

Marua had not slept properly for the last few nights. Her eyes were heavy with sleep, but she kept them open with a conscious effort. But in the end, her exhaustion won over her alertness and she drifted into a deep slumber. *Indumati* heard her regular soft breathing and decided that *Marua* had fallen asleep. She opened her eyes and looked intently at her to confirm that she was asleep. The jackals howled in the mango orchard in the backyard. *Indu* realized that it was past midnight. This would be the right time to go ahead with her plan, she decided. Very slowly, careful not to make the slightest noise, she climbed off the bed. Once again, she looked at *Marua*, still not sure if she was really asleep or was feigning. The feeble flame of the lamp that stood on a lamp-stand flickered casting grotesque looking shadows on the wall. *Indu* tiptoed to the door and released the bolt from the socket noiselessly. She stepped outside, turned and cast a furtive look at *Marua*. She knew that it was only *Marua* who could foil her plan at the last moment. Heaving out a deep sigh she moved ahead closing the door behind her. She had never moved about in the palace alone and unescorted in the dark of the night. Time and again her feet got tangled up in each other. Though the path leading to the door was familiar, she stumbled a few times but kept on, guided by a strange determination. Her insides were shrouded in morbid darkness as the outside world was plunged into the same pitch-black midnight. Her heart fluttered at every little sound. She was startled at the sound of a bat flapping its wings, the scampering and the scurrying of a mole or a mouse, and even at the wind that rustled through the trees. Her whole body trembled in the fear of being discovered by somebody. What an irony of fate! The princess, who ruled over the palace, was afraid of the maids and the servants! But the truth is that when a person intends to violate divine orderliness, he or she is bound to be afraid. A hundred maids and servants of the palace housed were sound asleep. Their cacophonous snoring sneaked through the chinks on the doors of their rooms. *Indu,* assured now that no one was awake to stop her, groped her way to the backdoor of the palace. She opened the door, took a deep breath and closing the door behind her walked towards the river.

The river swelled with the floodwater. The currents rushed on at great speed like the unstoppable Time. The water touched the lower steps of the bathing *ghat. Indumati* stepped into the water. Bubbles whirred up as she waded through the deepening water level. The sound of a soft splash was heard, and then there was total silence. The amber moon sank on the western horizon. The moon that went down the western skyline would come back up the next evening. But the moon that went set in the river, the moon of *Samsharpur* palace, would never rise again.

CHAPTER - 40
MARUA COLLAPSES

A person with a mind haunted by unknown fear rarely enjoys sound sleep. Even the faintest sound jerks him awake. Excess exhaustion and several sleepless nights had driven *Marua* to sleep despite her efforts to remain awake. The loud voice of the night watchman snapped her awake. At the strict orders from the zamindar, the night watchmen kept vigil in turns since the number of thefts and burglary had gone up. As *Marua* was slowly drifting back awake, a night watchman called out loudly, "Be aware!." The call was instantly followed by the howl of a pack of stray dogs. *Marua*, startled, groped about the large bedstead with a sleepy hand but contacted nothing. She sat up abruptly and peered at the side of the bed where *Indumati* usually slept. The bed was empty. She jumped off, her eyes darting around the room. The lamplight had dimmed and she pushed out the wick in the lamp to brighten the light. Her heart in her mouth, *Marua* looked under the bedstead. Then she pulled away from the bedspread and flipped about the pillows. Her nervous eyes darted around the room, to its dark corners. But there was no sign of *Indumati*. Her heart skipped a beat as she looked at the door. It was ajar. But she was sure that she had bolted the door shut before going to bed. Her head began to whirl— blank darkness engulfed her. Her mouth turned dry. She tried to scream but no sound came out. She opened the bedroom door wide and rushed out to the courtyard. Darkness reigned everywhere. *Marua* rubbed her eyes hard and looked around. Nothing! She trembled like a tender stem in a storm. She ran towards the backdoor that led to the bathing *ghat* on the riverbank. To her utter dismay, she discovered that the double doors were open. Collecting all her strength she began to scream— "Help, help someone please— everything is lost—." A thick dark veil shrouded her vision as she slumped on the ground and lost consciousness. Some of the maids who had been sleeping lightly recognized *Marua*'s voice. "'It is the elder princess *Marua*." They came out screaming, "What is it? What happened?" By then the loud uproar had awakened everybody. They banged their doors open and hurried outside to see what the matter was. The panic-stricken maids and servants bumped against one another as they ran towards the backyard. No one knew what had happened. The zamindar *sa'anta*, disturbed by the hue and cry strode into the inner quarters of the palace. "What is all this? What is going on?" Who would answer him? No one knew for sure what had happened. Suddenly a woman's eyes fell on a white figure lying by the door. She let out a loud cry pointing at the figure. Everybody, jostling one another, ran to the place where the figure lay. The zamindar also moved towards the spot. A maid looked closely and shouted, "It's the elder princess *Marua!*" Everyone began to talk at once adding to the confusion. "Quiet," the zamindar snapped, "Someone gets to the bottom of this."

"Get some water and a fan," someone shouted. A maid sprinkled water on *Marua* 's face and another fanned her. *Marua* opened her eyes and looked around searchingly.

Before anyone could ask her anything she blabbered, "*Indu—Indu—Indu—*." It was only when *Marua* uttered the name, the absence of *Indumati* hit everyone with the force of lightning.

Where was Her Highness *Indumati*? The servants and the maids quickly brought lamps and began searching for her. *Indumati* was nowhere in the palace. The zamindar, taking a group of barber-boys who held flaming torches, walked towards the riverside. On the wet ground, two well-shaped and small but distinct footprints were visible. They went towards the river and disappeared. An uncontrollable shudder ran through the zamindar *sa'anta's* body. Had not the barber-boys held him back, he would have fallen on the muddy ground. No one spoke. Tearing apart the silence the zamindar wailed, "Alas, my darling daughter! My precious!" By dawn, the news had traveled to all the houses in the village. In every house, people lamented the loss of their darling princess.

CHAPTER - 41
A GODDESS APPEARS IN THE RIVER

River *Sapua* flowed past the length of the backside compound wall of the palace of the zamindar of *taluka Dashagram*. Just below the compound wall were steps leading to the bathing *ghat*. This bathing *ghat*, built exclusively for the use of the habitats of the inner quarters of the palace was a restricted area. No outsider was allowed admission there. At about seven hundred meters west of the bathing ghat was another bathing *ghat* which was meant only for the young female folk of the *Karana* caste. The male folks of the village were forbidden even to pass by that place, be it day or night. The zamindar's palace was in the middle of the village. There were other *ghat*s in both directions of the palace but at present, we will not dwell upon the descriptions of those *ghat*s since they do not have much relevance in the present context.

The night was about to depart. The village was draped in a thin, transparent veil of darkness. Suddenly a huge uproar erupted at the bathing *ghat* for the young female folk. Startled by the loud screams that traveled to the village, the elderly women rushed towards the *ghat* to see what happened. Young and old women in their curiosity and hurry bumped against one another ignoring all propriety of relationships. The young women, their water pots cradled in their arms stood gaping at something at the root of the Banyan tree. The thing looked like a beautiful idol of some goddess. "Goddess Ganga has appeared in person!" remarked the elderly women. There was a relatively intelligent woman who dismissed all the speculations and said, "You are all wrong. She is our mistress the *sa'antani*. She has metamorphosed into a goddess" Women began to blow conches and sound auspicious ululations in veneration of their *Sa'antani* who had turned into a goddess. A flock of women lay prostrate in the damp, muddy ground in reverence while some stood motionless, their palms joined. Another group, the end borders of their sari wound around their necks, prayed to the goddess to cure the ailments their children suffered from. Some newlywed brides silently prayed for the early return of their husbands from their workplace to the village. The male folk, curious at the noise hurried towards the bathing *ghat*. In their eagerness to find out the cause of the uproar, men and women, jostled and bumped against one another ignoring all propriety and respectful limits of relationships. To the right side of the steps on the bathing *ghat* stood a huge Banyan tree. Year after year floodwater had swept away the soil beneath its thick twisting roots on the right side making them hang in the air a little above the water level. An idol of the goddess Ganga had remained stuck in a bifurcated root. Her arms rested each on one side on the prongs of that root. The tapering ends of the root, one on each side jutted out towards the river. The goddess stood there, her lower half from waist to feet immersed in the water. During the rainy months, floodwater rushed into the tributary rivers without warning and receded as quickly as it entered. Perhaps the effigy of the goddess had come floating about while the river was filled with floodwater. When the water receded, the effigy had remained stuck to the root of the tree. The waterweeds entwining the effigy thwarted back the current of the water which retreated forming foamy whirls. It looked like a garland of white-water lilies encircling the waist of the goddess. On the forehead of the goddess, just over where she wore the vermilion spot, dazzled a diamond. The sunlight filtering through the foliages of the Banyan tree glinted off it diffusing a rare iridescence. The tiny gem-studded rings that adorned her curly tresses that went arching about her forehead towards her ears on both sides of the diamond flashed colorfully creating an impression of a resplendent rainbow. Both hands of the goddess were placed on her bosom. She wore gem-inlaid rings on all the five of the champak flowers like fingers of her right hand. Gold bracelets and gem-studded gold bangles adorned her arms and hands. The big pearl nose-stud she wore radiated in the broken sunlight. Her back was completely covered by the length of her thick long hair that went below her waist and floated about in the water. A few tremulous locks partially covered her beautiful face. Like someone strewing pearl beads from above, water dripped from the leaves of the tree on her lovely head.

The male folks were equally vociferous in their speculations about the appearance of the goddess in the river. "The effigy has come floating in the current of the river. It must be the artistry of one of the best sculptors in Cuttack," one of them, with a keen imagination remarked. "Can't you see how he has burnished it with cinnabar and yellow orpiment to give it the color of the champak flowers. Look at her nose. How beautiful and sharp like the edge of a sword! And her eyebrows!! As if a skilled painter has drawn them with a brush, arching them perfectly on both sides to touch the ears! The silk sari is tightly wound and knotted around her slim waist preventing the possibility of floating away in the strong currents of the river."

None of his listeners bothered to reason out how an effigy could have come floating this far from Cuttack in one piece. "How very beautiful the goddess would have looked had the effigy not been smeared with mud," said a few. "And look, her face with her eyes shut has tilted to the right. Reclining in that position the goddess looks even more beautiful. As it sways slightly pushed about by the water current, the effigy looks like a living goddess."

The morning worship of Lord *Binod Bhari* was being performed in the temple amidst the blowing of conches, drum beats and jangling of cymbals. The zamindar *sa'ante* of *taluka Dashgram* sat praying in front of the deity. Disturbed by the loud uproar at the bathing *ghat* he stood up and strode towards the spot. The head priest and his assistants: the errand boys and the ones who held aloft the flags of the Lord and those who played the drums and jangled the cymbals ran after him. As the zamindar approached the *ghat*, the crowd parted making way for their master. The zamindar stared at the flood washed figure of the goddess. "O Lord *Gobinda!* What is this? Is it a new sport of yours?" The zamindar strongly believed that nothing in this world occurs unless lord *Gobinda* willed it. He is the supreme source of virtues and vices, of glory and disgrace, of gain and loss! We, humans, are just puppets in his hands. He makes us dance according to his own will.

Suddenly they heard an ear-splitting outcry. All eyes turned in the direction from where the sound came. About twenty men, smeared with mud, came out to the open. Their bodies were drenched from the rains of the night before. They whined and screamed —-

"Look there, our princess!!" They kept on repeating the words in utter agony pointing at the half-immersed figure.

"Find out who these men are! What is that they say about the goddess being their princess?"

When questioned, the men said that the daughter of the zamindar of *Samsharpur* had drowned in the river last night. Her body floated away in the strong currents of the floodwater. They had taken five boats and been searching for her all night and at last, had found her here.

The zamindar heaved out a deep sigh. "O Lord *Gobinda*, may your wish be fulfilled," he said. He turned to look at his people and added, "Look, she is my son's bride, the daughter-in-law of our family. Do not do anything undignified." All the male folk averted their eyes off the goddess figure and immediately left the *ghat*. The maids from the palace ran to the riverside to see Her Majesty, the bride of their *kuanr sa'anta*.

Everyone except the brides of the *Karana* families whose husbands were alive was asked to leave the place. The *Karana* brides started preparing for the final journey of the *kuanr Santa's* bride by blowing conches and sounding ululations. They decked the bride gorgeously with new silk clothes and ornaments. It is a custom in Odia families to strew flowers, coins, cowries and fried paddy flakes on the way in which the funeral procession of a *Karana* bride having her husband alive, moves. Accordingly, baskets of flowers, fried paddy flakes, coins of various denominations, cowries were fetched from the palace for the funeral procession. As it was customary, a barber-woman had clipped the nails and a small length of the dead bride's hair. The *Karan* brides collected the nails and hair to treasure them as auspicious relics. It was almost noon by the time all these rituals were over. The horse rider postman who had followed the men from *Samsharpur* had ridden away to pass the news on to the zamindar of Samsharpur. He had returned along with an important *Karan* of *taluka Samsharpur* via boat oared by four boatmen carrying a submission from the zamindar. The *Karan* from *Samsharpur* palace fell at the feet of the zamindar of *Dashagram* and prayed tearful in eyes, "Your Majesty, the zamindar of *Samsharpur* has made a humble submission at your kind feet: 'She is no longer the daughter of his family but the bride of yours,' he had said. You must see to it that the funeral rites that befit the bride of your family tradition are appropriately performed. His second request is that the ornaments she wears must not be removed."

"O Lord *Gobinda* may things happen as you wish them to—-" said the zamindar of *Dashagram* three times. With a heart heavy full of sorrow, he ordered the *Karan samantas* to see that the rites were duly performed.

The final journey of the virtuous *Indumati*, whose name meant as beautiful as the moon, to the other world, had ended before the moon came up in the sky.

CHAPTER - 42
THE GENERAL HOSPITAL

In the middle of a large airy room on the first floor of the Cuttack General Hospital there stood a bedstead fixed on iron planks. A coir bed was laid on it. There was a soft, cotton stuffed quilt that was spread over the mattress along with a few pillows. There was one large from on the north side and one large door on the south side of the room that leads to a long corridor outside. In between the two doors, there were two large windows that overlooked the corridor. Another relatively small door led to the next room in the east. A young man lay motionless in the bed covered in a clean, white sheet. Doctors stood by the bed examining the patient. They put a thermometer under the patient's tongue at short intervals to see if there was a drop in his body temperature. The patient had been lying unconscious with a high unremitting fever for the past nine days. The temperature remained at a constant 105 degrees. His servant, a barber boy, sat by the foot of the bed night after night. When sleep overpowered him, he just took a light snooze resting his head on the board at the foot of the bedstead. Doctor Beams, the civil surgeon, and his assistant Doctor Sukanta Ray made several visits a day to examine the patient. A couple of interns kept watch on the patient's condition all day and all night in turns and reported it to the doctors. The young servant did not understand anything about medical science, but tears streamed down his eyes as he watched the doctors examining his master. Sleeplessness and lack of food had taken a toll on him and he looked like a skeleton. One could notice the ribcage under the skin that now looked like dry parchment. He had become so weak that it was difficult for him to move his limbs, but he completely ignored his health. His sole attention was focused on his master's recovery.

On the tenth day of the patient's admission, the doctors came early in the morning to check the patient. They measured the fever and found that there was a significant fall in the temperature. It had come down to 102 degrees. The patient moaned softly and there was a slight movement of the limbs. The doctors looked at one another. The young barber guessed that there was some change in the patient's condition. A deep sigh of relief heaved out of him. The doctors were both happy and surprised at the loyalty and love of the servant for his master. "Don't you worry any more *Saita*," said the doctor sahib, "your master will be all right." *Saita* burst into tears. Sukanta Ray, the Assistant surgeon, cleaned and dressed the patient's wounds. He made him drink down some warm liquid and left. The compounder was given directions to feed the patient the same liquid every two hours.

CHAPTER - 43
RECUPERATION

The fever came down slowly but surely. Following the doctor's advice, the patient now took a short walk in the mornings and evenings along the corridor with the support of a walking stick. The wounds on his body had almost healed. The Civil Surgeon treated him with all sincerity. But it was the great care and deep concern of the Assistant Surgeon Doctor Sukanta Ray that did the miracle. Doctor Sukanta Ray had hardly left the patient's side since the day he had arrived from *Samsharpur*. The doctor was a good-natured person, a gentlemanly and greedless character. He usually did not collect consultation fees from his close friends and the patients who were not financially well off. He was more concerned with the patients' recovery than his own fees.

This patient was however neither a close friend nor was he a poor fellow. He had learned that the patient was the sole inheritor of the zamindari of the *pragana* of *Ashureshwar*. The huge *pragana* would be led to a condition of disorder and anarchy if something happened to the patient. The news of the sad demise of *kuanr GovindChandra* 's mother and wife had reached the hospital in time. But the patient, at that time, was unconscious with a high fever. The doctors with mutual consultations agreed that news of the death of his mother and wife might move him to a state of shock. Important *Karanas* from both zamindaris had taken a couple of houses on rent and stayed near the hospital. They collected reports from the hospital and sent them to the zamindars of *taluka Samsharpur* as well as of *taluka Dashagram* via the mail runners in the mornings and evenings. But they were not permitted to meet the patient. The hospital people were particular that *Saita* shouldn't know about their presence at Cuttack. The true-blue servant too had no interest in anything except the recovery of his master.

CHAPTER - 44
SAD NEWS

The darkness of the evening was beginning to settle. Electric lights were on in all the rooms of the hospital. *Kuanr Govind Chandra* and Doctor *Sukanta Ray* sat talking in the *kuanr's* room. The young doctor, for the last few days, was keeping *Govind Chandra* engaged in light conversations to relax his mind. *Saita* was busy making the bed.

"Doctor, I heard loud wailing and screaming from the ground floor, what happened?" asked *Govind Chandra*.

"Oh, that! An indoor patient, who was a landlord in some village died. He had been suffering for a long time from a critical disease. He had consulted several Ayurvedic physicians and got himself treated by them. Finally, he came here. But it was too late. He passed away early this morning. His kinsmen and acquaintances were mourning," the doctor said.

"Doctor, what does your medical science say about rebirth?" asked *Govind Chandra* after a thoughtful silence.

"Well what exactly do you mean?" the doctor asked wonderingly.

"I want to know if there is life after death."

"Look, my friend, we doctors deal with the mortal body of a man, his biological constitution. Your question relates to spiritual philosophy. It is about faith and religion. As far as my knowledge goes, the sacred texts of all religions admit the truth of the immortality of the soul. Men with no idea of religious philosophy too accept the theory of the immortality of the soul. Even the empiricists admit this truth."

"But the disciples of *Charvak* declare that the soul gets destroyed along with the human body. Their epicurean philosophy prescribes that one must try to derive maximum pleasure from life at all costs. They say that there is no returning once the body is reduced to ashes."

The doctor let out a burst of derisive laughter. "Haa! Haa! Men of wisdom had years ago denounced and derogated the epicurean philosophy of *Charvak*. That evil theory had long since gone extinct. Such atheists happen to appear on the surface of this earth every so often. Defying the existence of God! I have no idea what happens to them in the other world. But such unlucky people suffer a lot in this life. You might for once trust the species of serpent or devil but never trust such deplorable preachers of hedonism. The hearts of such men are totally bereft of all human values and compassion for the suffering of humanity. Their sole objective in life is to achieve their own selfish end. They can stoop to any level of criminality to attain material pleasure and prosperity. It is just the fear of the law that holds their evil instinct in check. Let us not dwell any longer upon the evil thoughts of such evil souls and turn our attention to the pious and righteous men and the preaching in our sacred scriptures. Didn't I tell you that all religious texts of the world agree on this point of the immortality of the human soul? Death only transfers the soul from one body to another. Look what the *Srimad Bhagavad Gita*, the sacred which is acclaimed worldwide as one of the best, says in this context:

Vasamsi jirnani yatha vihaya
Navanu grhanatinaro'parani
tatha sarirani vihaya jirnany
anyani samyati navani dehi

As a person puts on new garments taking off the torn ones or shifts to a new house abandoning the old one, the soul moves into new a mortal body, giving up the old and worn-out one.

Jatasya hi dhruvo mrtyur
Dhruvani janma mrtasya cha
Tasmad apariharye' rthe
Na tvam sochitum arhasi

Death is inevitable for the one who has taken birth. Birth is certain for the one who dies. Hence, you should not lament discharging the duty which is unavoidable.

Dehino'smin yatha dehe
Kaumaram yauvanam jara
Tatha dehantara-praptir
Dhirastatra na muhyati

As the embodied soul continually passes in this body, from boyhood to youth to old age, the soul similarly passes into another body at death. The self-realized soul is not bewildered by such a change.

We find many explanations of this in our sacred texts. Death is not an end, it is only a transformation. We shall follow the ones that die today and be united with them in the afterlife. Men of wisdom, therefore, forbid the lamenting the dead." The doctor paused here and looked intently at the *kuanr babu. Kuanr Govind Chandra* who had noticed the doctor fumbling and looking at him several times as he spoke, guessed that he was preparing the ground for saying something more important. At that moment, the doctor gripped *GovindChandra*'s right arm tightly and said, "Look here, my dear friend, I have bad news for you—your mother—-"

Kuanr Govind Chandra sprang out of the chair and screamed – "What? My mother is no more?!!" he began wailing. *Saita* rushed to him — "Oh *Maa Sa'antani*!" he let out a loud sob clutching at the feet of his master. He had wept several times earlier when his master lay sick in the hospital bed, but he held his sobs in check since it was a public place. But now he cried loudly throwing away all propriety.

After a long time, the *kuanr* stopped crying but the sobs still choked his heart. The doctor wiped the *kuanr's* face with a handkerchief soaked in water from time to time solacing him with soothing words. *Saita* lay keeping his head at his master's feet.

The senior doctor, before returning to his bungalow had advised Doctor *Sukanta Ray* not to keep the patient in the dark any longer. The sad news of the death of his mother and wife had to be broken to him. Seeing the condition the *kuanr* was in, Doctor *Sukanta* could not summon enough courage to reveal to him the news of his wife's death. But he would be answerable to his superior the next morning unless he did so. He had to leave everything to fate and take the risk, he decided. *Kuanr Govind Chandra* sat speechlessly. The doctor motioned the ward boy who brought some liquid tonic in two glasses. With some effort, the doctor managed to make the *kuanr* swallow the liquid. In a similar process, the tonic was poured into *Saita's* mouth. Without letting him know it, the doctor felt the *kuanr's* pulse and to his relief found that his condition had stabled. With much reluctance, and with great effort he spoke a little loudly to make him audible to the patient,

"Death of one's mother is very painful, but she had lived her life—but——"

he stopped abruptly. *Kuanr Govind Chandra* raised his eyes to look at the doctor. He stared at the doctor's face. The doctor said in a small voice, "Could the death of the wife be more painful than that of the mother? ———"

"What? My *Indu*! — My *Indu* too——?" a loud scream escaped the *kuanr* and he fell on the floor, unconscious. The doctor and some of the other employees of the hospital lifted and put him in the bed. *Saita*, who had fainted too, was made to lie down on a mat on the floor. The doctor along with eight interns and a few employees of the hospital kept watching over the patient's condition all through the night.

CHAPTER - 45
PENITENCE

A graveyard silence hung over the palaces of the zamindar of *Ashureswar pragana* and of the *taluka Samsharpur.* Everyone, be it man or woman, was in a state of shock. Since the eventful day, zamindar *Baishnaba Charana Patnaik* had given up all interest in worldly issues and spent his days in the temple of the family's tutelary deity Lord *Gobindajiu.* With a prayer shawl wound around his neck, the zamindar sat in front of the deity silently praying. He had not uttered a word in days. Today, after taking his morning bath, clad in the wet clothes, he went to the temple again. Standing with his palms joined in reverence in front of the deity he spoke his heart out.

"O Lord *Gobinda*! You are the Lord of my life! You are the Supreme Lord of our family. Our ancestors have served at your feet through many generations. I am but a slave at your holy feet. But I was blinded by false pride. I claimed myself to be the gem in the crown of the *Srikaran* class and the king of the land. My huge material property made me heady and I have derogated and demeaned people. But O Lord, all men and women in this world are your children. Your divine justice would never have let my arrogance and pride go unpunished. You smote my pride and reduced it to dust. O Lord! Reduce me to the dust at people's feet. Rid me off all worldly bondages and make me concentrate upon serving at your holy feet. O Lord of my life, O Merciful One! Forgive the wrongdoings of my son. You have brought him to earth with the purpose of carrying forward the name and glory of our family. Make him too a slave at your feet. He had fallen into bad company and violated a moral code. You have meted out his punishment to him. But now forgive him O Lord! He reaps the consequences of my own evil doings. I now relinquish all the property I have made and all wealth I have amassed. They are all yours. Please relieve me of my worldly engagements and take me back to your divine abode, my permanent home. O Lord! Take mercy on me and grant my wish!!"

The night before, the zamindar *sa'anta* had his will prepared by his trusted lawyer. He lay prostrate on the floor and put the sealed envelope at the deity's feet. The gist of that will was:

"All the movable and immovable property of our family is a gift from our tutelary deity Lord *Gobinda*jiu. Now I offer all that property at the feet of the same Lord and prepare to leave for another world to atone my sinful act. All the people the palace houses will earn their livelihood serving the Lord. I also hereby declare that my only son will live his life as the Lord's servitor and earn the basic amenities for his living from the property of the Lord through the services he rendered to him."

There in the *taluka Samsharpur*, zamindar *Sankarshana Mahanty* lay in his bed like a lifeless body since the death of his daughter. He did not exchange a word with anyone nor did people even the ones closest to him could gather courage enough to console him. It was only his trusted *Srikarana Ramahari Mahanty*, who looked after him.

On that day, zamindar *Sankarshana Mahanty* got up

from the bed as if he had retrieved his strength. He summoned the important and senior *Karans* of the village. Everyone was sitting in the temple premises of Lord *Binod Bihari* holding their heads down. The zamindar *sa'anta* sat quietly. His face did not reveal any expression, neither of joy nor of sorrow. There was pin-drop silence. No one even dared to take a deep breath.

The zamindar *sa'ante* looked at the people, let out a deep sigh and said, "My brothers, you know that everything in this world happens at the will of the Supreme Lord. Still, men reap the consequences of their own doings whether good or bad. You have seen yourself how two important and prestigious families have suffered the disastrous consequences of my wrongdoings." Some elderly and senior *Karan* men with folded palms, tears brimming in their eyes remarked, "No, Your Majesty, you have not committed any offense. All that has happened is decreed by the inexorable Providence."

Things do not happen your way despite your efforts, and even if you do not put in any effort the inevitable takes place.

Marua had started recovering slowly, but since the day the *Sa'ante* left the palace renouncing his material belongings, she had again relapsed into a depressed mood. She sat in the large shabby bedroom which she shared with her dear *Indu* looking at the beam of its ceiling with vacant eyes. When she became conscious of the reality around her, she recollected the events of that night with a heart heavy full of remorse and penitence. "I am responsible for the disaster. It was on account of my own fault that I have lost princess *Indu*, my dearest friend. Had not my cursed sleep taken me in its evil grip, she would not have been able to leave the room. The sin of my negligence must be atoned. I will follow the path my dear princess has taken."

Some of the clever and alert maids in the palace who observed *Marua's* restlessness, her furtive glances and her frequent visits to the bathing *ghat*, became apprehensive of *Marua 's* intention. They kept a watch over her activities day and night.

Meanwhile, *Sadananda babu* was upset at the unexpected turn of events. "How unfortunate!" he said to *Rajivlochan* as they discussed their failed plans. "How hard we had worked to plan a good future for *Govind*. He had gained a wife like the goddess Saraswati. He was about to inherit a huge zamindari without any effort of his own. But the man spoiled everything with his stupidity. Not only did he put himself in trouble but spoiled the whole game. How, by using our manipulative genius, we had planned out things! But we suffered a serious setback because of that fool. We did not get even half of what *Sankarshan Mahany* had promised us. Damn him! Damn his stupidity!"

While *Govind Chandra* lay in the sickbed all day and night, *Saita* sat by the foot of the *kuanr's* bed attending to him. He had not cared to eat or sleep properly. As he sat gloomily, his cheek resting on his palm, he cursed himself for his own neglectfulness. "Alas! It is because I had not taken things seriously. I knew I smelled the whiff of a conspiracy by the evil *Sadananda babu* and *Rajivlochan babu*. Now my master has to go through all this pain. I should have informed the zamindar *sa'anta*, his father as soon as I doubted their intention. My young master is a simple, guileless man. He had fallen into the trap set by wicked men. O, God! Please let my master recover from his illness. After that, I will atone the sin I have committed by ignoring things and causing such trouble to my master."

CHAPTER - 46

Time never waits for anyone.

It flows on incessantly carrying the joys and sorrows, pains and the pleasures of the world on its currents.

It had been more than ten days since the *Kuanr* had suffered the shock of the news of the death of his mother and his wife. Though he was slowly coming out of shock, the hospital authorities had not given him permission for his discharge. The *kuanr* showed no interest or disinterest in either remaining in the hospital or leaving it. People are normally alarmed by the thought of a disaster. But a disaster makes a man stronger and helps him know the real nature of other men. It is through the experience of a disaster man understands the ways of the world. A strange and grim calmness had settled over the *kuanr*'s mind these days. He no longer distinguished between pain and pleasure, neither between a friend and a foe. He interacted only with his trusted valet *Saita* who remained with him like a shadow. His thoughts were focused on *Inddumati* whose image remained glued to his heart. At times he felt a bit restless remembering his dead mother. He barely responded to the employees and ward-boys of the hospital. He only spoke to *Saita* when there was a need to talk to him.

An arrangement was made to send the wages of the servants and other domestic help at the Cuttack residence along with the money to be sent to the masters for their individual expenses. Every time the expense money for the masters came from the palace, the servants' money came along with it. The practice was still followed with regularity. After sending money to his old mother and meeting his own meager expenses *Saita* could still save a reasonably large sum from his wages. He usually got the surplus money converted into gold coins and kept them in a pouch which he carefully tucked in the folds of his waist-cloth. He had only touched the money to meet the hospital expenses when his young master was hospitalized. *Saita* had never bothered about expenses, nor did he keep count of the amount he was spending on his master's expensive medications or diet. He did not bother counting the money the hospital-boy returned to him after collecting the required items from the market. *Saita* had only one objective, one wish—to get his master fully cured. God eventually listened to him and the young *kuanr* got around. In the process, however, *Saita's* pouch had been emptied. But the expenses had not stopped. Had it been the palace or even the residence at Cuttack, the shopkeepers and vendors would not have been so rigid about immediate payment. However, here in the hospital, immediate payment in cash was a must. *Saita* had not given into a difficult situation. He had a great hope that once he went out to the town and met the friends of his master, they would immediately come to his rescue and his financial troubles would come to an end. He knew that the master's friends like *Ramkrishna babu, Sishu babu, and Lakshman Babu* had on several occasions borrowed heavy amounts from him. They would, before even *Saita* opened his lips, volunteer financial help. But at that very moment, a disturbing thought crossed his mind. None of these friends of his young master, who frequented his house in his good times had paid a single visit to the hospital. Hadn't they heard of his master's sickness by now? *Saita* wondered. He was anxious to verify the genuineness of these friends. He told his master, the *kuanr babu* that he had some work in the town and left the hospital.

Saita knew that the elder master *Sadananda babu* had come to their residence at Cuttack. But he decided to check the facts out. He inquired from the neighboring houses and learned that the elder *Sa'anta* had been appointed the *Naib* of *Harihar Mardaraj*, the zamindar of *Pargana Delang* in the district Puri four days ago and had left for his new station. They said that the *Naib* would receive a salary of a hundred rupees a month.

Saita knew about this newly appointed zamindar of *Delang*. The estate of *Delang* was under the custody of the government when he was a minor. The young zamindar had studied at Ravenshaw Collegiate School and passed Matriculation in the third division. He was admired as a fine orator and addressed several student-assemblages. He wrote poems too. People in his contact said that there was a deposit of more than a lakh rupees in his name in the government treasury.

He was a close friend of Sadananda *Babu*. The estate was returned to *Harihar Mardaraj* when he became twenty-three. He appointed his friend *Sadananda* as the *Naib* and took him to *Delang*.

Failing to meet the elder brother *Sadananda, Saita* decided to try the other friends of the *kuanr*. He went from one to another, but they frankly and rudely avoided him. "Who are you and why have you come here?" asked *Siba babu*. "Go away! I don't have time to listen to your problem." These *babus* regularly visited the *kuanr* and spent long hours with him. *Kuanr Govind Chandra* had spent a lot on treating these so-called friends. But now, *Saita* thought in distress and anger, they refused even to recognize him! There was no point in expecting any financial help from such ungrateful, unscrupulous men.

Disappointed and without thinking where he was going *Saita* walked towards *Manik Ghosh Bazar*. As he walked past the sweetmeat shop of *Rama Sahu* holding his head low, *Rama Sahu* recognized him and called out, "O, *Saita Barike,* hey brother! Why are you going away like this? Please come to my shop for a while!"

Saita did not want to discuss his master and his troubles with anyone in the town. He avoided people, especially those he knew closely. But it was not easy to ignore *Rama Sahu.* So *Saita* went inside. *Rama Sahu* greeted him and pushed out a sitting board made of the wood of the mango tree. *Saita* sat down on the sitting board. *Rama Sahu* moved a little closer to him. At that hour of the day, there was no customer in the shop. The errand boys were also not there. He cast a furtive glance around to see if anyone else was listening. Assured that only the two of them were in the shop, he asked, swallowing, "*Saita bhai,* is it true what people say? That the *kuanr sa'nta* went to the zamindar's palace to thieve?"

"That's a lie, a dastardly lie," *Saita* protested vehemently.

"Then why is he kept in the hospital under arrest?"

Saita tried to explain that the hospital housed only the patients and not thieves or dacoits. Even the patients involved in criminal activities are kept in the hospital for medical treatment. Later they were sent to jail. But the *kuanr sa'anta* was in the hospital because he was sick.

Rama Sahu responded, "Yes, now I can understand."

"But why did you ask such a thing?"

"Please do not take offense but I was curious to know. While your elder master was staying in your Cuttack residence, I used to carry his snacks and sweetmeats there regularly. The elder master and his friends spent the evening hours in gossiping and merrymaking. One evening I went there to ask for my payment for the refreshment I supplied from my shop and I happened to overhear your elder master telling the other young men about the *kuanr sa'anta*.

'*Govinda* had stolen a lot of jewelry from his father – in-law's house. As he ran away in the darkness the guards of the zamindar's palace captured him and thrashed him mercilessly. Later he was handed over to the police. It is a serious issue. We must never be seen in his company. The police will arrest us as abettors of the crime. Let him suffer the consequences of his doings. Why should we involve ourselves in it?'"

Saita sheds copious tears at this baseless accusation made against his innocent master. He looked emaciated and pitiable. Shopkeeper *RamSahu*'s heart melted with pity for this faithful and sincere vassal. He forced *Saita* to eat some snacks and sweetmeats in his shop. *Saita* drank a pot-full of water after consuming the food and lay down on the floor for half an hour or so, thoroughly exhausted.

CHAPTER - 47

It was past midnight. Silence reigned in the hospital. When the need arose, resident doctors and interns stayed the night to attend serious patients. But there was no such patient on that night. The interns had gone to sleep in their respective rooms. Only soft moaning sounds were heard from a few beds.

The *kuanr* had not gone to sleep. He had been sitting on the bed, lost in thoughtful silence. *Saita*, as it was his habit not to go to bed till his master fell asleep, sat on the floor, by the foot of the bed. That morning while they did their rounds Doctor Beams Sahib and Doctor Susanta Ray had remarked that the *kuanr* was now completely cured and was fit to leave the hospital. He could go to the palace anytime he wanted. *Saita* was delighted at the news. He was relieved to find his master speaking and moving normally. *Saita* was interested to go to the palace but could not bring himself to ask the *kuanr*. The *kuanr* talked to him for a long time on different subjects. "You have been put to a lot of trouble on account of me," he said. "What to do? It was all preordained. We, puny creatures, do not have the mind to fathom the inscrutable ways of Providence. Just the way the pureness of gold is determined by putting it in the fire, a friend's loyalty is tested in the hours of crisis. You are intelligent enough to understand the ways of the world.

You must deal with all sorts of difficult situations applying your own mind. There is no point in blaming others for the ill-luck that befalls us. I have something to ask of you. You have never disobeyed my orders. It will hurt me if you do that now."

Saita clutched at *kuanr GovindChandra's* feet and broke into tears. "Your Majesty, why do you speak like this? You have never said such things to me in all these years."

"Now, don't you worry so much and do as I say and don't ever tell anyone about it," said the *kuanr*. "Get me the yellow-colored tin trunk and the small iron-casket." *Saita* brought out the boxes as he was asked and put them on the bed.

Kuanr GovindChandra unlocked the boxes. He took out two heavy necklaces each having five strands, a pair of gem-studded bracelets, five diamond-studded rings, and some other expensive jewelry and put them all except one ring, in the small iron-casket. He slid the ring in his index finger. It was a simple ring, with no diamond in it. But the ring had the name *Indumati* engraved on it. As the *kuanr* transferred the ornaments one by one to the iron-casket the light from the lamp diffused off them and made luminous patterns on the walls. All these jewelry were offered to him as a gift by his father-in-law.

Govind Chandra had written a note earlier and kept it under his pillow. He took out the letter and handed it to *Saita*. "You have to go to the moneylender *Lachman Bhagat* tomorrow morning and get five thousand rupees from him in exchange for these ornaments. And mind you, the transaction should be extremely confidential. Bring the money only in the form of gold coins and paper notes."

"Your Majesty, *Lachman Bhagat* will lend the money just by your asking him to do so. What is the need for keeping this valuable jewelry in his custody?" *Saita* asked, joining his palms respectfully.

"You don't seem to understand. Why should I carry the jewelry wherever I go? It will be risky. Let them be there with him, safeguarded."

The next evening the moneylender came in with the amount. He greeted the *kuanr* respectfully and shed copious tears pressing the edge of his dhoti to his face. *Saita*, too, could not check his own tears. He went out of the room, again and again, to wipe them away. But the *kuanr sa'anta* sat on the bed in silence, there was a look of calm resignedness over his face. The moneylender was puzzled at the blank, expressionless look of the *kuanr*. He handed the money to the *kuanr* and bowing his respects once again, left.

The *kuanr sa'anta* took out paper notes amounting one and a half thousand and gave them to *Saita*. He also gave him a diamond-studded ring. "Give five hundred rupees to your mother from this," the *kuanr sa'anta* said. "The other one thousand rupees is for your marriage expenses. Keep this ring always with you. Here, take this sealed envelope and keep it carefully. Open and show it to the ones who question you about how you came to possess the money and the ring."

Saita was reluctant to accept such a huge amount from his master, the *kuanr*. The ring was too expensive to be in the possession of a poor barber boy like him. Perhaps the master is giving me all these as a token of appreciation for the services I have rendered during his illness. But what I have done was my duty. There is no need for such gifts. But my master will feel hurt if I refuse to take them. Let them be here with me for the time being. I shall see later what can be done to return them, *Saita* decided.

"Leave for your home before dawn tomorrow. Give the money to your mother and ask her not to worry about me anymore since I am all right now. She will be a little relieved at the news," the *kuanr sa'anta* said.

Saita felt disturbed. Though the *kuanr sa'anta* has recovered, he was still a bit weak. He did not want to leave him out of his sight even for a moment. But he did not have the heart to go against his master's will. His village *Mukundapur* was *only* about thirty miles from Cuttack.

"I will hire a two-way boat from the ferry *ghat* of *Hariharpur*. Since the boat will move downstream, I will reach the ferry *ghat* at my village before sunset. My house is close to the riverbank. I will call a little loudly and my mother will know that I have come. I will spend the night at home and start early in the morning carrying half a seer of beaten rice. I will make the return journey in the same boat and get back here by the next evening or a little later. It will not be a big problem." *Saita* planned his journey accordingly and bowing at the feet of his master got ready to leave.

CHAPTER - 48

Every morning, as soon as he reached the hospital, Doctor *Sukanta* climbed up the stairs to the first floor and went to *kuanr Govind Chandra*'s room. He spent nearly an hour in examining the patient, checking his medicines and diet chart. Even after the *kuanr* had recovered he still maintained that routine. That day too, like on all other days, the young doctor went up to the first floor. From a distance, he saw that the door of the *kuanr's* room was ajar. It was something unusual. By this time *Saita* would, after assisting his master in his morning routine, open the doors wide and sat outside waiting for further orders from *the kuanr.* That day Doctor *Sukanta* missed the inevitable presence of *Saita*. Wondering what the matter might be he called out a bit loudly in English, "Hey, friend! Sleeping in this morning are you?"

Silence greeted him.

The young doctor, his mind in the hold of some uncanny fear, tiptoed towards the room. He opened the door a bit wider and peered inside. Putting his head further through, he craned his neck and looked in the direction of the bed. The bed was empty. He opened the door wide and stepped into the room. He looked closely around. The bed was neatly made. The clothes hung neatly in the closet. Even the utensils which the *kuanr* used were placed on the shelf. Everything looked neat and orderly in the room. But there was no sign of either the *kuanr* or *Saita*. Suddenly his eyes fell on the envelope on the bed. It was a large-sized envelope and was so placed on the bed to catch easily one's eye. The doctor picked up the envelope. It was sealed at different places. To his surprise, he discovered that the letter was addressed to him. Quickly he tore open the flap and took out the letter from inside. He began to read,

"Om! May my soul find shelter at the feet of Lord *Sri Hari!*

Dear Friend,

Please accept my respectful greetings. We have been friends for about five years now. You know everything about me. You are now not only the savior of my life but also the one who guides my sinning soul towards the path of redemption. Though I have made many friends in Cuttack you are only indeed the one true friend who has advised me on morality and righteousness. You know my nature. At times you got vexed with my unreceptive attitude and exclaimed, 'The atheists claim themselves to be too wise to listen to good advice from anyone.' I used to laugh away and ignore your good words during those days. But now I repent every moment for that. I don't know how reading a few English philosophical texts had made me so arrogant to doubt the existence of God. What a foolish, ignorant man I was to believe the atheists who challenged the infinite power of the Supreme Soul, His endless mercy that spreads about in the whole cosmos. We experience it every moment in our lives but prodded by our limited knowledge tend to ignore it. Four years ago, when I suffered from brain fever you had saved my life. Since then, you have been advising me on moral principles and to have faith in God. But ignorant men without any steadfast aim and with a disordered manner of living take pride in defying moral and spiritual advice. I could still recollect what you said about the attitude of atheists. 'The atheists could stoop to any level of sinfulness, they only desist themselves from doing that for fear of law.' You were very right my friend! The atheists who always seek selfish pleasure are neither interested in nor are able to experience the pain people around them pass through. I am a burning example of the sort. I have proved myself a foe to my father. I have killed my mother. I am responsible for the death of an innocent angel-like maiden.

Friend, there is not an atonement that might commensurate with my sin. As I am reminded of one after another the hideous crimes I have committed the flame of remorse and repentance scorches my heart. My life is absolutely shattered. Everything has fallen apart. Only death can bring rest to my agitations. But I would not add to my sins by ending my own life in my own hands. I now surrender myself at the feet of the Supreme Lord. I will take his name in my heart and spend the rest of my life visiting the holy and religious spots. I know that my sin has its limitedness but the Lord's mercy is endless, infinite. Hence, I have a strong belief that the Lord will take pity on me and forgive my evil doings. I am prepared to accept the most difficult punishments if the Lord wishes not to forgive me. Let him smite this sinning soul of mine and redeem it.

My dear friend! Now I realize that man has no power to battle or counter the inexorable. His false ego and vanity motivate him to believe himself to be a free and willful creature. But the inevitabilities of life steer him to certain paths whether he wished it or not. The limited knowledge and poor rationales of humans always admit defeat before the mysterious power of destiny. But it is true that faith in

God, righteous temperament and patience help men to withstand the terrible tragedies of life.

I have also come to realize my friend, that if the sinner makes a total surrender at the Lord's feet to seek redemption for the sin he knowingly or unknowingly commits and promises never to indulge in any form of sinful act in his lifetime, the Lord will surely take pity on him and redeem his soul. The Lord's feet and his mercy will henceforth be my only sustainer.

My friend, you will find paper notes of two thousand rupees inside this envelope and gold coins amounting to one and half a thousand rupees from under the pillow. I, with all humbleness, pray you to give the two thousand rupees to the doctors. The rest one and half thousand you distribute among the employees and interns in a manner as you deem proper. They have taken a lot of pain and nursed me during my illness. To tell the truth this is only a humble return for the services they have rendered.

In the end, I will request you not to take any pain to look for me. It will yield no results.

Your friend *Govind Chandra*

Doctor Beams arrived and learned about the *kuanr's* disappearance from Doctor *Sukanta Ray*. In an informal meeting it was decided that the money *Govind Chandra* had donated to the students would be used to buy textbooks for the poor students. Doctor Beams, in consultations with others, employed a team to start the search for the *kuanr* in possible places.

CHAPTER - 49

Nothing remains permanent in this world except for the permanence of change. A place where a festive atmosphere prevails today could suddenly and without notice be usurped tomorrow by distress and woe and may be filled with cries of agony.

The palaces of the zamindars of *Ashureswar* and *Samsharpur* where the sun of happiness had set forever were now enveloped in black despair. The kinsmen and relatives on both sides lamented the irrevocable loss for a long time. But nature has its own means of mitigating the severity of the pangs of sorrow. 'Forgetfulness' like a soothing balm comes flowing in the currents of Time and spreads itself over the lacerated heart. Had it not been so, humans could never have survived through the constancy of pain and agony. In course of time normalcy is restored to the shocked and shattered lives of the mother that loses her son or the young woman who loses her husband. Sometimes, even a semblance of a smile could be noticed on their faces.

The subjects in both the *taluka*s were slowly getting over the sorrow. Time had draped a screen of forgetfulness over their memory of the mishap that had befallen their respective landlords.

It is a common practice of the subjects to discuss their powerful masters behind them. They talk about the virtuous nature, the judiciousness, the philanthropic bent of mind and generosity and other good and evil qualities of their masters at their back. Often it is seen the subjects denouncing their all-powerful masters while these masters are alive. But rarely people derogate a dead man of similar socio-economical status. Even if a person was evil during his lifetime, people try to recollect only his good qualities after his death. Only rivals with a narrow mind and mean nature tend to besmirch the name of a dead man.

A popular saying goes that 'trouble never comes alone'. There are times when trouble coming in different forms and shapes overwhelm human beings. *Kuanr GovindChandra* suffered serious physical pain for a negligible and minor fault of his. To add to the physical suffering, he was to suffer the agony of his noble name being disgraced. He was baselessly and falsely accused of the crime of thieving. The rival party derived a lot of malicious pleasure when the *kuanr's* family suffered the agony of disrepute while the friends and relatives of the great family held their heads down in abject humiliation. But the serene light of truth cannot remain concealed for long under the flimsy darkness of a lie. Hence people now lamented the sufferings, the insult, and injury the *kuanr* had to pass through and his self-imposed banishment. The people of all the villages in the *pragana of Ashureswar* and all the *Srikarana* groups had by now clearly understood the malevolent role played by the shrewd *Sadananda* in letting such a mishap befall the family. The poor and orphan boy whom the zamindar *sa'anta* and his compassionate wife had treated as their own child had betrayed their trust. He was at the root of everything. The entire society of the *Srikarana* s has turned against him. So angry were they with the devilish *Sadananda* that they would not have hesitated in the least to take his life in their own hands. Nor would they have considered it a sin. The poor, widowed mother of *Sadananda,* not able to bear the shame and disgrace her son brought upon her, had died long since.

Sadananda, now convicted as a thief by the court of law, was put behind bars. On learning about the anger of the people and their desire to avenge the wrongs committed by him, *Sadananda* was sure that he could not find shelter at Cuttack on his release from the jail. A sinner repents his sin when he suffers the retribution. Diehard and seasoned criminals without moral or a sensitive bent of mind may be different, but it is obvious that intelligent and educated persons like *Sadananda,* who commit a crime for the first time in life and was punished for it, would be plunged into the depth of despair. In such moments of despondency and self-abuse, it is natural that they would contemplate some form of penance.

CHAPTER - 50
THE BOWER-HUT

Regardless of the joys and sorrows of people, time flows on at its regular pace. Four years have passed since the tragedy had devastated the peace and happiness of the families of the two zamindars.

At the extreme limit of the sacred city of *Brindavan*, by the side of river *Yamuna* and away from all other such large-sized ones there stood a comparatively small, shabby-looking bower-hut. The hut was seven by five feet by area measurement. It had a slanting, thatched roof. A few tatty planks of wood joined together formed the walls of the hut and a bamboo-screen served as its door. A length of rope held the bamboo screen door fixed to its position. Theft and burglary are, as we know, are rampant in the cities and towns, especially at the pilgrim-spots. But the thieves and their kindred had dismissed this place from their area of operation since there was no point in taking the pain of visiting the place. In the name of property in the hut could be listed a few earthen pots and dented utensils, a tattered grubby mattress, a pot made of the empty shell of a bottle-gourd. There was also a small water pot having more than one hole which were sealed with lac to prevent the water from flowing out and a stack of palm –leaf manuscripts. A clay pot filled with the earth where a holy basil sapling was planted stood in one corner of the hut.

It was time for lighting the evening lamps. A little before the evening worship in the temple was about to begin, a monk came out of the hut and walked towards the temple of Lord *Gobindji,* holding his head down. He was about fifty years of age. He had a loincloth wound around his waist. He had also wound a prayer shawl that was torn and knotted at several places around his head. He wrapped the upper portion of his body with a prayer shawl that had Lord *Gobindji's* name painted on it. Usually the monks and ascetics of *Brindavan* carried a string of prayer beads or sling-bag with them as they moved out. But this ascetic held nothing of the sort. He just kept on repeating 'It is all your wish O Lord *Gobinda,*' and walked on, his eyes downcast. He reached the temple just in time to have a *darshan* of the Lord's evening worship. Then he lay down prostrate on the floor and said his prayers. After that, he performed the usual ritual of going around the temple.

As he circled the main temple, he sang the prayer:
Victory be Thine O Lord Gobinda ji
The creator of this universe
The dweller of the devotees' heart
Of joy ultimate, you are the source

O' Lord Madhusudan
O' the source of Absolute Joy
It is You O Lord, who all fear and
It is you who all the sin in
The heart of a man does destroy;

The Supreme Ruler, Savior of our souls
The One who smites the wicked ones' pride
In our journey across the world
That is like a stormy sea
You are our Supreme Guide;

I salute at your feet O Omnipresent
Redeemer of our sins, the Supreme One
That causes our existence.

Singing such prayers, he offered worship at the smaller temples of deities like *Gopnath ji, Madanamohan, Shyam Sundar,* and other deities at the monasteries in the temple premises. Then he came out of the temple and walked back to his own hut. As he came out of the temple another *Vaishnav* monk about the same age and with similar get up, walked after him. But the second monk carried a folded blanket over his shoulder and a saffron-colored bag under his left arm. He held a walking stick in his right hand and moved slowly after the first monk. As the first monk reached the door of his hut, he could sense the presence of someone behind him and turned to look. In the clear moonlight, he saw a monk-like figure who looked vaguely familiar. The man who had followed him came to the front and fell at his feet. He clutched at his feet and touching his head to them wept fitfully. 'O My Lord! Please forgive me! O My Lord! do save me!' –the second monk cried out. The first monk looked down and found that the man who lay at his feet was a *Vaishnav* monk. He took two quick steps behind afraid that he was committing a sin by making a *Vaishnav* monk touch his feet. 'Ho this is a *Vaishnava* monk! Please get up! Oh, what a sin I have committed!' He bent down and tried to raise the man holding both his arms in both hands. 'No no, I am not a *Vaishnav*,' cried out the man who lay on the ground. 'I am a slave of a *Vaishnav* like you. I am a sinner, a vermin, and an unforgivable criminal. I am your slave, *Sankara Mahanty*.' Now the first monk, who was the zamindar of *Pragana Ashureswar* recognized the other monk. He was the zamindar of *taluka Samsharpur*. The zamindar *Baishnaba Charana Patnaik* knew that *Sankarshan Mahanty* also had renounced his home and property and had become a monk. He embraced him fondly and said, 'Ho brother *Shankar*! Come in.' Both men stood embracing each other for a long time. *Shankarshan Mahanty* said brokenly, 'My lord, Your Majesty! I know I have committed such sin which can never be atoned. I have traveled to several holy spots like *Puri, Rameshwar, Haridwar, Dwaraka,* and *KashiDhama* but a visit to all those sacred places could not bring me peace of mind. But now that I have touched your feet I feel greatly relieved.'

The small hut stood by the riverbank. Both men washed their hands and feet in the water of the river and went inside. As it was his daily routine to sit praying for some time after returning from the temple, *Baisnaba Charan Patnaik* began singing prayers. The other monk, zamindar *Sankarshan Mahanty* sat with joined palms, listening to the prayer.

Later they each ate a little of the food offerings made to the deities and sat down on the floor. After a pause, the first monk asked, 'What was that you were saying *Sankar bhai*?'

Sankarshan Mahanty once again touched his head to *Baisnhab Charan Patnaik*'s feet and said with abject humility, 'Your Majesty, you know everything. It is because of me that you have renounced the world and are living the life of an ascetic. I too have lost my only child, my daughter, forever. There is no atonement for the sin I have committed.'

The first monk sat in silence for some time, his eyes closed.

'Brother *Sankarshan*,' he said after a while, 'Everything in this world occurs at the will of Lord *Govind ji*. Not a blade of grass will move unless he wills so. We, human beings, carried away by a false vanity claim that we do everything. *Gobind ji* is the sovereign Lord of the universe. We human beings are only his agents who carry out his will. In the *Karma Yoga* section of *Srimad Bhagavad Gita* it is said clearly:

Prakruteh kriyamanani gunakarmani sarvashah
Ahamkara bimudhatma karta aham iti manyate

(The bewildered spirit, under the influence of the three modes of material nature, thinks himself to be the doer of all kinds of activities, which are in actuality carried out by the directions of The Supreme Lord)

Eshwara sarvabhutanam hruddesheh Arjuna tisthati
Bhranayan sarvabhutani yantrarudhani mayayaa

(The Supreme Lord is situated in everyone's heart O' Arjuna,

And is directing the wonderings of all living entities who are seated as on a machine made of material energy.)

The great poet *Tulsi Das* writes:

Suna Bharat kala prabal biloki kahe muni natha
Sukha dukkh janam maran jasa apajasha vidhi hath

Time is the most powerful, O Bharat
The joys and sorrows of human beings
Their births and deaths
Their fame and disgrace, everything

Is in the hands of the Supreme Lord
Who writes their destinies.

You must have experienced it yourself that whatever we hope to happen hardly happens while which is most unexpected happens. Who is at the root of all these? It is the Supreme lord. He has created all of us. We are his children. Will God, our Supreme Father ever want to bring any harm to us? No one knows what is going to happen in the future. We puny human beings, grieve at certain painful things that occur in our life without trying to look into the truth. But if you think you are responsible for the present condition of mine, I will consider you as my benevolent friend. I must offer my gratitude to you for taking the blame.'

'You must understand brother that we have to perform two duties in this life, one to our body and the other to our spirit. The body is perishable, but the soul is immortal. Man must always put in his best efforts to elevate his spiritual essence. One must indulge in the task of benefiting human kind and society following the path of truth and justice as long as his body and mind are strong and capable. That is why God has sent us to this earth and that's the way we can uplift our moral status. As the body parts weaken with the advancement of age, we must direct our thoughts towards our spiritual redemption. The sacred texts, hence, advise us to adopt the austere practices of an ascetic severing the domestic and worldly ties. The same thing is prescribed in the holy text of *Srimad Bhagabata* that one must sever the domestic ties and proceed on a spiritual journey at a certain stage of life. The Creator of the Universe had ensnared us human beings in a web of illusion. It is not easy to cut through the web and come out. Though man realizes that truth and piety are the major sustainers of his spirit, he always craves the worldly pleasure. His interest in earning virtues is not as keen as his interest in amassing wealth.

I have heard several times the learned *Kulamani Vidyabhushan,* who is an important member of the Assembly of Pundits, quoting from *Samkhyayoga* and explain that desire is the chief impediment in the path of the redemption of the soul. The Great Gautam Buddha, whose heart melted at the miseries human beings have to pass through, felt through his meditation at the bank of river *Niranjana* that our desire is at the root of all forms of sorrow. But human beings, blinded by illusion are not able to do away with their desire and passion which is the root cause of their woe. But noble and saintly souls easily free themselves from the grip of desire and pursue the path of truth and righteousness. At times certain unexpected events happen in a man's life which fills his heart with such dispassion for the worldly life that he snaps all ties with it and chooses for himself a life of spiritual austerity. Just think that if such a mishap had not befallen our families, we would have remained entangled in the clutches of our vanity, ego and selfishness. The sinful thoughts and actions would have been prodding our spirit further and further to its doom. However, I have not neglected my religious duties even as I was shouldering my domestic responsibilities. I have worshipped at the feet of the Lord and said my prayers regularly. The little virtue earned through such an act had not gone in vain. It is His grace that has enabled me to renounce the world and dedicate myself completely to the service of the Lord. So now my brother, come let us spend the rest part of our lives in this sacred spot, in the company of saintly souls serving at the feet of the Supreme Lord. Let us surrender ourselves at His feet. Let His wish be fulfilled.'

'Your Majesty, I am an ignorant, impious fellow. You are my mentor and my Guru. Please guide me on the right path. I will spend the rest of my days here as your disciple,' said *Sankarshan Mahanty.*

The elder monk, *Baishnaba Charana Patnaik* said, 'Brother, what more do I know than you? What advice and what guidance I can give you? Lord *Gobinda ji* rules supreme over our lives. Let us surrender our virtues and vices, our joys and sorrows at His feet and be free of all worries. The Lord Himself advice in *Srimad Bhagavad Gita:*

Sarva dharman parityjyam mam ekam saranam braja

Aham twam sarva papebhyoh mokhsyayishyami ma suchah.

(Abandon all forms of religion and just surrender yourself to me. I will absolve you from all your sins)

Khsipra bhabati dharmatma shaswachhanti nigachhati

Kaunteya pratijani hi name bhaktam pranashyati

(He quickly becomes righteous and attains lasting peace, O' son of Kunti; declare it boldly that my devotee never perishes.)

CHAPTER - 51
THE NEW SERVITOR

The two monks lived a blissful life in the hut at the bank of river *Yamuna*. They had snapped all cords that connected them to worldly life and spent their days in taking the Lord's name. Every day, after the morning worship of the deities at the temple they collected alms from seven specific houses. They cooked the rice and pulses and vegetables thus collected and ate one meal in the evening. In the night they recited *slokas* from *Srimad Bhagabat* and *Bhagavat Gita*.

A young mendicant offered his services to these two sanyasis for about two years. He was a young man, with long, dry and oil-less, wind-blown hair who wore an ochre-colored loincloth around his waist like a *Vaishnav* monk. Nobody knew a thing about this new arrival, nor about the purpose that brought him there. After the two monks went to the river to take bath in the early hours of morning, this young man swept the open space around the hut. He also mopped the floor of the hut with cow-dung mixed water. He brought water in a water-pot from the river and put it in the hut. He completed all these works before the monks returned from the river and went away. He bowed at their feet and touched the dust at their feet to his head if he chanced upon them and walked away quickly. There were some servitors in the holy city of *Brindavan* who offered their unasked-for services to the sadhus living there. The monks thought that the young man might be one such servitor. But each of the two felt that the looks of the young man were somehow familiar. But they did not disclose this to each other. The monks usually spent time praying and taking the Lord's name and did not talk much with each other. Though they had met the young man several times they had not asked him to tell them about himself. They also did not want the young man should offer his services for free. They had asked him through gestures not to do so many works for them, but the young man went away from the place feigning he did not understand what they said.

CHAPTER - 52

It was the eighth day of the dark lunar phase in the month of *Bhadrav*. The air was festive in *Brindavan or BrajaDham* because it was the day of the celebration of Lord Krishna's birth. The city bustled with new arrivals not only from the common households of the city and places outside of it but also devotees of several classes of the *Vaishnava* community. There were large crowds in every temple, and it was very hard for the devotees to enter the temple premises and have a *darshan* of the deity. The sky was overcast since morning. There were a few light showers too. By evening layers and layers of rain-swollen clouds had spread across the sky enveloping the city in thick darkness. The light from occasional flashes of lightning helped people to find their ways to their respective destinations.

Though the time of Lord Krishna's birth was at midnight, worships and prayers had started in the temples, in the bowers, huts and in the houses of people since evening. The recital of cantos from Srimad *Bhagabat* had also begun.

On the floor of the small bower-hut on the bank of *Yamuna* sat the two monks on two cloth-mats. On a small wooden stand was placed the sacred *Srimad Bhagabat* opened at the page where the tenth canto began. It was adorned with flowers and sandalwood paste. Before it, different fruits and sweetmeats were laid out on leaf plates as offering to the sacred, divine text. There was no scarcity of alms in the holy spot of *Brindavan* on that festive occasion. Pious pilgrims and rich householders, on this holy occasion were giving away fruits and sweetmeats in large quantities for the offerings at the temples as well as for the *Vaishnav*s and other pilgrims and devotees who had arrived from different places. It might be because of the crowdedness of the place on that day or the sufficiency of such fruits and sweetmeats obtained from charitable people, the two monks had not gone out to collect alms. The royal families who came on pilgrimage and other benevolent persons sought out the bower-huts where monks stayed and sent large quantities of uncooked food there. Hence, there were lots of such food items in the hut where these two monks lived.

In the hut, the younger monk was reciting lines from the tenth canto of *Srimad Bhagabata* and the elder one was listening, his eyes closed.

Suddenly a frantic knock sounded at the rickety door and someone called, 'Someone kindly help me, my life is in danger!' The younger monk stopped reciting and both looked at the door in surprise. The frantic call for help sounded again on the other side of the door.

'Brother *Shankar,* open the door kindly. The guest must be in some trouble!' said the elder monk. 'We are fortunate enough to have a guest at the threshold of our shabby hut.' The monk opened the door and the guest entered in slow, hesitant steps. Both the monks looked fixedly at the guest. The guest was a young man but looked wan and emaciated. He wore tattered, grubby clothes and had long matted hair and an unkempt beard. He held a small water pot by its handle in his right hand and a stick in the left. The nails on his fingers were not clipped perhaps for a long time and had become unusually long. There hung a threadbare blanket across his shoulder. It appeared that he had got drenched in the rain a short while ago. Water dripped from his hair and the blanket and he shivered from time to time. 'Brother *Shankar*, our guest has got drenched in the rain. First, get some water for him to wash his feet and then give him some dry clothes to change into,' said the elder monk and resumed taking the name of Lord *Gobinda* as was his habit.

The younger of the two monks recognized the guest. The guest fell down at his feet like a tree that was felled. 'Your Majesties, my father, and father-in-law, I am *Govind*, your sinner son, the wretched villain.'

The two monks had now no doubt about this new guest's identity. The elder monk sat in solemn silence, looking steadily at the young man, his eyes filled with tears. The younger monk sprang to his feet and embraced the guest, crying out, —'*Govind*, O my dear son *Govind*!' He wiped the young man's body with a bathing-napkin as he called out his name, tears trickling down his eyes.

'Brother *Shankar*,' said the elder monk, 'take him to the river so that he can wash. There was a large water-filled pot in the hut, but the saints have touched them. That water should not fall on *Govind*'s feet.'

Govind Chandra took a bath in the river *Yamuna* and changed into dry clothes. By that time the younger monk had put some logs of wood in the hearth and *Govind Chandra* began warming himself with the heat of the fire.

The recital of *Srimad Bhagavad Gita* resumed. After the episode of Basudeba carrying baby Krishna in a basket over his shoulder and putting him in *Nanda* 's house in

Brajadham or Brindavan ended, the recital stopped. The sacred text was worshipped, and offerings of fruits and sweetmeats were made in the Lord's name. After the worship was over the three devotees helped themselves to the *Prasad* and went to sleep.

CHAPTER - 53
IDENTITY REVEALED

Like all other days, as it was their routine, the two elderly monks went out to river *Yamuna,* chanting the name of the Lord, carrying two small pots of water by their handles. The young guest was still asleep. Long, strenuous walks along the roads of *Brindavan* and the drenching in rain had exhausted him. *Braja Dasa,* the fellow who had been doing the job of sweeping and mopping and getting water for the monks during the last few years arrived at the daybreak. As it was his regular practice, he took the broom and began to sweep the front -yard. While busy at the job, he heard a voice from inside the hut.

'O Merciful Lord! The voice sounded so familiar!'

Braja Dasa was startled and looked about eagerly to see the owner of that voice. Slowly the door of the hut opened, and a young ascetic came out. *Braja Dasa* cast one glance at him and fell at his feet. Clutching at the feet of the young ascetic he cried out in a loud voice.

'Ho! Leave my feet,' protested the surprised young ascetic. Then he looked closely at the fellow. And then a look of recognition sparked in his eyes. 'Hey, you, *Saita!*' the young ascetic exclaimed and raised the fellow holding both his arms. 'How have you reached here?'

Saita and his young master had not seen each other for more than five years, but both the master and the servant recognized each other instantly. The young ascetic asked Saita repeatedly how he came there but *Saita* sobbed hard and words choked his insides. He was not able to speak out a single word. Surprisingly, the young ascetic stood calmly, without displaying any emotion. After a moment, he sat down and pulled his trusted servant by his hand and made him sit by his side. 'Now tell me *Saita*, how have you happened to come here? Where have you been all these days? Is your mother all right?'

It took *Saita* some time to calm down. He began to speak haltingly: 'Master! On returning from my village I could not find Your Majesty in the hospital. I searched desperately for you in all possible places at Cuttack for three or four days but in vain. I went to most of the nearby places like the sacred towns of *Puri*, and *Bhubaneswar*, to the caves of *Khandagiri*, *Udayagiri* and so on. My mother, on hearing the news of Your Majesty missing constantly shed tears. Then she fell sick and became bedridden. She never recovered. She kept the money which you had asked me to give her in a pouch under her pillow and prayed for your wellbeing. When she became very ill, she gave me back the money-pouch and asked me to spend them on worshipping different deities and offer the *Vaishnav* saints food and clothes. She thought that doing so will bring her the news of your wellbeing. During the days that followed, her condition worsened. I had got her treated by two village physicians but there was no improvement. Shortly before the end came, she stopped taking medicines. She just touched the medicine to her forehead and kept them down. For about ten or so months I sat by her side nursing her. At last, in the morning of the eleventh day of the bright lunar phase of the month of *Kartik*, she passed away.'

'You have done right,' said *Govind Chandra* regretfully.

After all, the world does not have even one such son like me who has killed his mother! He breathed out a deep sigh. A few drops of tears of remorse trickled down his eyes. *Saita* quickly changed the subject.

'I performed the funeral rites of mother and started living alone in the house. One of those days the news of *elder sa'anta* being arrested reached me. I rushed to Cuttack to know if it was true. The elder *sa'anta Sadananda babu,* who had been appointed as the *Naib* to the young zamindar of Ratanpur was convicted in the charge of misappropriation of cash and was sentenced to two years imprisonment.

I was utterly disappointed. I left Cuttack and started looking for you. For about three years I searched you in pilgrim spots like *Rameshwar* and *Haridwar.* One day while I was wondering about the *Manikarnika* mountain pass, ten or so months before now, I heard a noise. It came from the bank of river Ganges. A couple of Muslim boatmen were heckling an ascetic. It so happened that a group of pilgrims had hired a boat from near *Rajghat* to reach the bank on this side. On arrival, all of them except the ascetic paid the fare to the ferrymen. 'I am a *sanyasi,* wherefrom shall I get money to pay the fare?' But the ferrymen won't leave him at that. One of the ferrymen punched the ascetic hard and shouted angrily, 'You swindler! Have you thought this boat to be the paternal property that you will journey in this free of cost? Why didn't you tell at the time you embarked upon it? You scoundrel! Give us the money!' The other boatman knocked him, and the poor fellow bent in double screaming out 'aah!' in pain.

I felt pity for the man and walked quickly to the spot. I had one *anna* with me tucked in the fold of my loincloth. I paid the fare and the ferrymen left. I looked at the *sanyasi*. He looked young. His hair was matted, and his body was smeared with ash. He wore a short length of ochre-colored cloth around his waist. He held a small water-pot by its handle in his right hand and carried a small bundle of ragged clothes under his left arm. He looked familiar and I peered at him closely.

'Hey, aren't you *Saita?* The *sanyasi* asked suddenly. I recognized him; he was the elder master! I fell at his feet. He looked so weak and emaciated. The ribcage was visible through the thin parchment-like dry skin. He was dressed like a beggar. His voice had lost its authoritative note and sounded low and dull.

'Where else should I have gone?' he said when I asked him what made him come here. 'You know everything. My sinful act had led two families of regal status to their doom. I am responsible for the death of my aunt, *Govinda*'s mother, and for the death of my own mother. I have decided to expiate my sin begging at such holy places. Rest I leave in the hands of Lord Almighty.'

Realization dawns upon the sinner when he gets deprived of even the smallest joys in life.

'It is from him that I came to know that both the old *sa'anta* are living here. He had somehow learned that Your Majesty would come here. I pinned my trust in his words and awaited your arrival. The Lord is very kind. He had, at last, brought me to your feet,' said *Saita,* in a voice suffused with emotion.

CHAPTER - 54
THE COMMAND

It was a little later after noontime. In the front yard of the bower-hut before the two old monks sat the young ascetic humbly with folded hands, holding his head down. *Saita* stood behind the old monks, his palms joined. 'Who is this young man, Govind?' asked the younger one of the two monks.

'He is *Saita,* father-in-law, sir!'

Saita had been, for the last year or so, working in the bower-hut. He used to come in the morning, sweep the courtyard, and mop the floor of the room and bring drinking water from the river. But the monks had never cared much to know about him. As for the older one he always walked to the temple holding his head down. It is only after the younger monk *Sankarshan Mahanty* came to the hut he had spoken to him on a few occasions.

"We have done whatever we thought we should have done for you,' said the elder monk, *Baishnab Charan Patnaik.* 'Now you are independent to follow any course of your own choice. But I somehow feel that you have not fully succeeded in obeying the commands of the Lord.'

Govind Chandra slumped at the feet of the two, and cried out:

'O, Father! My living gods! My ultimate mentors! I am ignorant, a fool. Being away from you had emptied me of all sense of duty, morality, and righteousness. Your Majesty! Kindly forgive the offenses I have committed and educate me with your advice on the right way of living.'

'My child!' said the older of the two monks, 'Keep this in mind – righteous living has two important aspects; all of us human beings are the Lord's children. The Supreme Lord will be pleased if we direct all our efforts towards the wellbeing of the society and for promoting healthy and wholesome living. The Merciful God Almighty has endowed us with some special virtues and commands us to use them for the good of the world. If we do not devote ourselves to this noble task, it will amount to disobeying the Lord's command. The Lord has kindly bestowed wealth, ability and knowledge inadequate amount upon you. You can use them to accomplish the purpose of serving the society in the right way. You must take the responsibility of performing the worshipping of the tutelary deity of the family as it has been done through generations. You have enough money to help the poor, oppressed and the downtrodden. You may elevate your spirit to a sublime level through the practice of austerity. But that will be a form of selfishness. Besides, if you live that way the virtues God has gifted you with will go waste.'

'*Govind*, my son,' said the younger of the two monks, 'I would also want you to follow the advice of my elder brother. You must shoulder the responsibility of the proper worshipping of the tutelary deities of both the families. You have also to see that the wards both the palaces have housed are being properly looked after. You are the sole inheritor of the properties of both the families. You must use the wealth discreetly to achieve these noble purposes. Now it is up to you to choose the right path and follow it.'

Govind Chandra bowed to the two monks, touched the dust at their feet to his forehead, and took their leave.

■■

GLOSSARY

Abadhana - a village school teacher

Abadhane - a respectful address for such a teacher or a senior

Apa - elder sister

Anna — coin used as currency in old times

Babu - a respectful address corresponding to sir; a native clerk or officer during the British rule

Bhadra - a lunar month corresponding to September

Bhai sa'aanta - respectful address for an elder brother

Bharavi - a Sanskrit poet

Brindavan — A holy city; modern Varanasi

Chandi patha - recital of mantras to appease Goddess Durga

Chhamukaran - an accounts clerk or treasurer (personal or official)

Cowrie - Kind of sea-shell used as currency during the British rule

Cutcherry - government offices and law courts collectively; A government or private office (a hall in a palace where such offices are held

Dhaangra- unmarried youth

Dhangri- nubile maiden

Dahi machha - the ritual of feeding curd and fish the ones going out on a journey to ascertain safety and success

Darshan –Have a glimpse of a deity in a temple

Doob — a type of holy grass used by Hindus in worshipping

Faye—Faye - a corrupt pronunciation of F.A (Final Arts)
Gandhari -Queen Gandhari was the mother of the 100 Kaurav prince in the epic Mahabharata

Ghat— a bathing place by the riverside; a spot by the riverside where boats are moored

Golam Mahanty - believed to be a low bred karana

Haat - A village market-place

Haribol - utter the name of Lord Hari

Jajnya - a Vedic sacrificial ritual

Jyestha - a summer month corresponding to May

Kadamba - A tree that grows yellowish, large fragrant flowers and has oval-shaped dark green leaves. (Lord Krishna used to play his dulcet standing under a Kadamba tree)

Karana - writer caste in Odisha; people who did ministerial jobs

Karma yoga - the preaching in Bhagavad Gita that prescribes that one must do one's duty sincerely without expecting a return

Kathjori - a famous and large river in Odisha

Kauravas - the progenies of the Kuru dynasty in the epic Mahabharat

Khadiratna - the surname/title of an astrologer who interprets birth-charts by drawing planetary cusps on the floor with a piece of chalk (khadi)

Killa Maidan- fort-field

Kuanr - the prince or the junior master in a noble family

Kunti - Queen Kunti was the mother of the Pandava brothers Yudhisthira, Bhima and Arjuna

Kush - a holy grass

Lilavati Sutra - a treatise of mathematical formulae written by Bhaskara

Mouza - a village being the unit of some houses, plots fixed for revenue purposes

Mukhtiar - a representative of a party in a court; a lawyer of the lowest grade; authorized agent

Muqaddam - a tenure holder under a zamindar

Neem - a large, sacred and medicinal tree with bitter-tasting leaves and buds

Paika - a warrior sect of ancient Odisha; a foot soldier, footman, peon

Pandava - the sons of King Pandu in the epic Mahabharat

Pausha - lunar month corresponding to December

Pargana - a large village

Prajapati - the celestial matchmaker for wedding (Lord Bramha)

Prasada - food offering made to a deity/deities

Raj Vaidya - an apothecary who treats kings and royal personnel or people of such noble status

Sa'anta - respectful address for a master especially landlord

Sa'antani - address from for the wife of the sa'aanta/the mistress

Samanta - feudal landowners/landlords

Samkhya Yoga — A section in the sacred Bhagavad Gita

Sana sa'antani- younger mistress

Saraswati - Hindu goddess of art and literature

Sastra - Hindu sacred scriptures

Shani- Saturn

Sloka - hymn from Hindu holy texts

Srikaaran - the superior category of the karana caste

Taluka - an estate; a revenue/fiscal sub-division

Utkal - the ancient name for the province of Odisha

Utkaliya - natives of Utkal

Vaidya - an apothecary

Vaishnav - a Hindu religious sect that worships Lord Vishnu

Yamuna - a holy river in north India

Zamindar - a feudal landowner (samanta/ sa'anta)

■